Ages of Love

(LOVE BY DECADE)

BY

GINGER SIMPSON

ISBN-13: 978-1495921582
ISBN-10: 1495921581

Electronic edition of *Ages of Love* published by:

Books We Love Ltd.
Chestermere, Alberta
Canada
ASIN: B00GXKW7OI

CHASTITY HOLMES
AGE TWENTY-THREE

CHASTITY

Her latest assignment had to be here someplace! Chastity Holmes rifled through the papers on her large mahogany desk. This wasn't her mess, but why wasn't she more organized? Somehow, her best intentions got buried under mounds of stuff despite her trying to change. No wonder she'd been given the nickname, "Chase." She'd spent her life in pursuit of everything.

Her shoulders ached with unaccustomed tenseness. She shrugged her left one, moving it in a circle to work out the kinks. Perhaps her new job caused stress, but she quickly shook her head and decided the most apparent reason had to be her recent celibacy. Obviously, not having sex had taken a toll.

Ending a relationship with her boyfriend, Eric, resulted in her accepting a position with Norwell Genetic Industries in Maryland—miles from California and her widowed mother. Eric had been a diversion, and she and her mother had drawn closer with him out of the picture. Still, a girl had to grow up, and moving and building a future away from home was often part of the journey to adulthood.

Although she'd shared two years of her life with Eric, their life goals didn't jive. The sex was fantastic, he had a successful career with an accounting firm, and wanted her to marry him, stay home and raise a family. At twenty-three, the thought of having kids boggled her mind.

They made an amicable split, and surprisingly enough, she hadn't shed a single tear. Maybe he hadn't been Mr. Right, after all.

Chase moved her right shoulder in the same rotation as the left, hoping the pain would go away. Why in the heck was she thinking about Eric anyhow? It wasn't like she didn't have anything better to concentrate on. She'd inherited a messy desk, piled with papers too long ignored. Obviously her predecessor had more organizational problems than she, so could Chase handle the challenge? She'd come here to build a new life and was on her own, far from anyone she knew. Wasn't it a little late to question her decision?

Taking a deep breath, Chase sagged back in her chair and took stock of her new office. The room was far more spacious than she'd expected, nicely decorated with matching furniture and new carpeting. A colorful landscape portrait of ocean waves crashing ashore provided a relaxing ambiance and all she had to do was look straight ahead. She'd expected to find a cubicle, so having a door with her name on it came as a pleasant surprise. Then, how come an empty feeling rose from the pit of her stomach? Although she expected some loneliness in a strange city, the damn picture reminded her of too many memories of walks on the beach in San Francisco with Eric. If it wasn't him she missed, perhaps the hollowness came from being miles from the place she'd always called home. She tipped her chin and focused on her desk.

The job came with a generous salary, but obviously lots of work. As a background investigator for all the applicants applying for research positions at Norwell, it appeared from the piles, her responsibilities were endless. She'd be checking the references of each applicant, doing a follow-up with their previous employers and digging into all the other relevant tiny details she might find. God, where to start?

Hard work didn't bother her, but finding a way to compact her job into an eight-hour day might, if she wanted some time to establish a life outside her office. Right now, the desk looked like no one had done anything except heap more paperwork to the stacks. Geez, did she have to do her own filing? She didn't recall seeing that in the job description, but fat chance she'd have an assistant.

Her mind wandered. Wouldn't it be wonderful to have a handsome, male aide to keep her organized and cater to her sexual needs? Thoughts of her imaginary assistant's hands roving over her body increased her respirations and yanked her back to reality. Upon attempting to straighten, she realized her hair, cascading over the back of her chair, had caught on something.

"Ouch." She squirmed and tugged until she freed herself.

Rubbing her head, Chase eyed the stacks on her desk. Enough wasted time. The last thing she needed was to be caught daydreaming. She reached for the pile of folders resting on the mahogany edge and they teetered precariously. Although she tried to catch them before they fell, the mountain cascaded to the floor in a colorful waterfall.

"Crap!" Chase chewed her bottom lip and sighed. She stretched over the desk and viewed the letterhead, pictures and reference correspondence littering the beige carpet.

"Okay dummy, if you'd taken time to organize things a little better and kept your mind on your job, you might have avoided this mess." But then again, maybe not. Too much snow always caused an avalanche.

She walked around and stood over the mess.

An unsettling face stared up at her from one of the photos on the floor. Damien Sloan, the newest applicant for the recently advertised Research Associate position. His file had been used as an example during her interview and was the very one she sought.

His smirking grin made her feel as though he peered up her skirt. She stepped to the side then realized her foolishness, but his leering expression still sent a shiver running through her body.

The warm temperature of the office overcame the chill and she shrugged off the blazer she wore. After hanging it on the coat rack, she hiked up her black sheath and dropped to her knees to gather the scattered papers. With Dr. Sloan's disturbing snapshot tucked back inside his folder, Chase crawled from one paper to another, sorting through the rubble, and returning each piece to its own file. The task seemed to take forever, but her newfound determination kept her focused. Never again would she let her desk get so cluttered.

With everything back in order, she leaned back on her heels and heaved another sigh. As she surveyed her new office from a lower perspective, she noticed the crookedness on the wall of the certificate that signified completion of her correspondence course. She made a mental note to straighten the frame and flicked away a stray wisp of blonde hair too close to her eye. Was that an elusive sheet between the file cabinet and her desk? She inched further under the furniture and extended her arm between the metal and wood but couldn't quite reach the paper.

Crouched, with her fanny in the air, she wedged her shoulder firmly against the desk and stretched her fingers as far as she could. "Damn, I can't reach it!"

Her office door opened and a cool breeze crept up her dress.

"Ahem." A deep throaty cough sounded behind her.

The shock lengthened her grasp and she succeeded in snaring the errant page, but a flush blossomed up her neck and set her cheeks ablaze. What a predicament—being caught in such an unprofessional posture.

She edged backwards, still clutching the paper, with her eyes charting the trail behind her. She focused on a pair of shiny black shoes, then sat back on her heels again and peered up into eyes as blue as a summer sky and clear as a mountain stream.

"Hell...hello there...."

Any explanation stuck in her throat as her gaze broadened to his stunning smile and wavy black hair, then drifted to massive shoulders and thick biceps incased in a blinding white dress shirt.

Her vision strayed to the zipper of perfectly creased slacks that encased a pair of very muscular thighs and remained there as if held by a magnet.

"Are you Chastity Holmes?"

His voice yanked her attention upward. He toyed with a tie that matched his eyes perfectly.

"Ah…yes, I am." She struggled to her feet with a distinct lack of grace and waved the piece of paper at him. "I was attempting to retrieve this stray document, and I'm afraid you caught me at the worst possible moment. I'm very sorry."

He shrugged and waggled an eyebrow. "No need to apologize. Whether that was truly your worst moment depends upon one's viewpoint."

"What can I do for you, Mr…?" Her burning cheeks suggested she change the subject right away.

"Blaine Logan…Detective Blaine Logan, of the Rockville Police Department." He squared his shoulders and appeared to stand at attention.

An immediate warning passed through her head. Police? Surely unpacking wasn't a crime. She pictured the full boxes lining the walls of her new apartment—something else that needed her attention.

"N…nice to meet you." She extended her hand.

Huge fingers encompassed her small ones, and although his palm was warm, a chill swept up her arm.

"Nice to meet you, too, Ms. Holmes…or is that Mrs. Holmes?"

Was this astonishingly handsome man flirting? Her gaze leapt to his finger, searching for a wedding band. Not even a tan line. She looked up and smiled, his piercing eyes causing her to squirm.

"So, Detective Blaine Logan of the Rockville Police, what can I do for you?" She washed away any notion of getting involved with someone in his line of work—far too dangerous. She motioned to the armchair next to him.

The leather crackled as he dropped his huge frame into the seat. He crossed his legs, resting an ankle on a knee and fixed her with a stare. "So, you didn't answer my question."

"It's Miss, but please call me Chase." She kept a very professional tone and expression.

"That's not usually a woman's name." He chuckled.

Chase tried not to scowl. She detested her mother's choice in names, but the nickname she'd acquired served her well. She motioned to the crooked certificate on the wall. "I'm officially Chastity Ann. My mother had a thing for C's. She named my brother Chance and my sister, Charity. Thank Goodness she only had three children."

He bit his lip, obviously to stifle another chuckle. "I'm sorry, I'm not laughing at your name, I just wasn't expecting to find someone as pretty as you named Chase."

"Fine, I'll forgive the snickering if you promise never to call me by my given name."

"It's a deal. Chase it is."

He adjusted his collar around the corded muscles in his neck. What other treats lay beneath this clothing? She exhaled, directing her breath upward to cool her heated face while she reached for a tablet on the desk. She fanned herself. "Is it warm in here to you?"

"Actually, I find the temperature quite comfortable."

"Oh…good. She attempted to mask her action by picking up a pencil to go with the pad, but disturbing visions of how he'd found her, crawling on the floor with her butt waving in the air, flashed through her mind. Thinking better of holding needless things, she leaned forward, resting her elbows on her desk. "So, Detective Logan…?"

"Please call me Blaine."

"Right! So, Blaine, what brings you to my office?"

He pulled up that same long leg and rested his ankle on one knee. She gaped at the size of his shoe and wondered if what 'they' said was true.

God, what was wrong with her? She leaned back in her chair, trying to wipe fleeting images through her mind.

"I understand you may be considering the employment of someone whose past I'm looking into. Does the name Damien Sloan sound familiar?"

At the name, her mind cleared and she sat bolt upright. "How uncanny! I had just put his folder back together when you walked in. May I inquire about your interest in the man?"

Blaine ran his forefinger across his chin. "Well, I can't tell you much, other than he's under investigation at the moment. At best, we only have circumstantial evidence, so what I need from you is his previous employment history plus any personal contacts he may have provided."

Picturing Sloan's evil face, Chase took a deep breath. "I'd love to help, but since I'm new here, I'll have to get authorization before I can release any information to you. I'm still unsure of Norwell's policies and procedures, but I do know that most of the applicant's data is confidential."

Blaine clasped his hands against his stomach and twiddled his thumbs. "I totally understand, but if necessary, I can get a subpoena."

Was he trying to impress her or sound threatening? She wasn't sure. Unfazed, she leaned forward. "I don't think a summons will be necessary, but I want to cover my own ass...assets."

Great! First she'd waved her assets at him, now she mentioned them. The heat returned to her cheeks. Hopefully he hadn't noticed her Freudian slip.

His smirk told her he hadn't. She wanted to slap the arrogant grin right off his face...or kiss him. What was it about the man? He elicited her most confusing emotions.

She stood on wobbly legs. "J...just let me step out and have a word with my supervisor. I'll be right back." Chase skittered for the door and didn't even look over her shoulder.

****

Chase returned to find Blaine standing behind her desk, straightening her certificate of completion. He squared it perfectly, then turned and faced her. "I see you've had formal training."

Was that a smirk? She walked around to her chair, assuming he would move out of the way. He didn't. Towering over her five-foot-five-inch frame, he stood directly between her and the desk. She didn't appreciate his disconcerting nearness and his condescending tone.

"Are you making fun of me?" She glared up at him, her defenses at the ready.

"Not at all." His tone lacked conviction.

"Well, you may not think a correspondence course is difficult, but earning a diploma via the mail is. I learned a great deal—enough to land this prestigious job." She made a sweeping motion of her office. "I doubt you have such lush surroundings."

He nodded. "I'm sure you're very good at what

you do." His tone smacked of patronization. "So...what did your supervisor say?"

Rather than engage in further rhetoric going nowhere, she drew in a breath. "Oh...I'm to fully cooperate with you."

The sooner she did, the quicker he'd be gone and she could return to some sort of normalcy. She pushed by him and took her seat.

He meandered back to his armchair and sat. "Great, I hate having to disturb judges. They can get so testy at times."

So, he hobnobbed with judges. Big deal! Could the man get any cockier?

She forced a smile. "So, Detective, how can I help you?"

Blaine glanced at his watch, then back to her. "I have another appointment looming. How about we meet for dinner later to discuss the case further?"

Despite his rugged good looks, her instincts screamed at her to say no. He was most certainly a male chauvinist and hadn't shown other than a hint of interest in her other than what she could do for him. Still, this was a chance to enjoy a free dinner and a night out. What could it hurt?

"Let me check my calendar."

She turned to her computer and purposely took much more time than necessary. Her days were filled, but sadly, her evenings were available. He didn't need to know that.

She spun her chair back around. "Luckily, it appears I'm free this evening...you did mean this evening, didn't you?" She cocked her head and smiled. "If you didn't, than I'm sorry to say I'm pretty well booked for the next couple weeks."

The lie rolled off her tongue like melted butter on hot popcorn.

"Tonight's fine. Do you have a favorite food?"

"Anything but fast food." Her answer came quickly. She'd been living on burgers since she'd arrived. Besides, he looked like he could afford to treat her to a decent meal.

"How about Mexican? I know a really great place."

All of a sudden, he sounded like a normal guy, making plans for a real dinner date. She raised a brow. Was this a façade? Did it matter? Tonight, he was only a meal ticket—albeit a good-looking one.

Her stomach rumbled at the thought of tacos and enchiladas. "Sounds good. I love ethnic food."

"Where can I pick you up?"

Chase scribbled her address down and handed him the slip of paper. "I don't live far from here, but I gave you my phone number in case you get lost."

He accepted the note. "I'm not likely to lose my way. I know the entire city." His virile good looks pulled at her attention...until he opened his mouth. "See you at seven?"

"Wow, the whole city." She couldn't ignore his cockiness again. "Seven is fine, by the way."

He stood, gave her a mock salute and left.

She sagged against the back of her chair and rubbed her temples where a stress headache loomed. What a day it had been so far. At least by agreeing to have dinner with Blaine, she'd get a chance to see if he was really as arrogant as he seemed.

Resuming an upright posture, she opened a folder. As creepy as this Sloan fellow appeared, she needed to review his entire file.

****

Chase ran a brush through her hair one last time, thankful for the length that made styling a breeze. She did a quick spin in front of the full-length mirror on the bedroom door to check herself from every angle. Navy-blue trousers and matching sweater fit her petite frame to a 'T.' The Rockville climate could get downright cold, but somehow she knew she wasn't going to be chilled tonight. Thoughts of Detective Blaine Logan warmed her despite reservations about his personality...and profession.

Ready, she eyed the line of boxes still waiting to be unpacked. Given her training, workload, and exhaustion, she'd barely had time to breath, let alone get fully settled. Besides, this really wasn't the place she dreamed of renting. The availability of vacancies had been the determining factor in her choice, and she ended up with a furnished place. Although she didn't have to shell out big bucks for new furniture, even her subtle improvements in curtains, matching throw rugs and a stereo system didn't hide the stains and wear. Those, coupled with the faint odor of previous tenants annoyed her. Every time she opened a closet, someone else's smell jumped out at her. Not a terrible scent…just not hers. Most likely no one else would notice, but because of her overly sensitive nose, she'd placed air-fresheners throughout the place. The disturbing traces of prior occupants faded a little more each passing day. Maybe by the time her mother paid a visit, she'd have the place looking pristine…or not.

The doorbell rang promptly at seven. Chase glanced down for a last minute check of her appearance and straightened the band on her sweater before opening the door. Hopefully her wide smile would mask her suddenly nervous stomach.

"You're right on time." She motioned him inside but he stood fast.

"I like to be prompt." Not so much as a hello. "I hate when people keep me waiting. Are you ready to go?"

She nodded. "If you come in, I'll get my purse."

He stepped inside and she walked toward the

bedroom. A 'gee you look pretty, Chase' would have been nice, but... Already he niggled her last nerve.

She reappeared with her shoulder bag. "Would you like to sit, or are we ready?"

He eyed the unpacked boxes. "Are you coming or going?"

"As I told you, I'm new to the job, and also to Maryland. Work is taking much more time and energy than I expected...."

"Where are you from?"

"Sacramento, born and raised."

"What brought you to the other side of the map?"

"An ad in the paper." She tired of his inquisition. "Can we go now? I'm starving."

"Sure, we can chat over dinner at El Corazon."

****

Sombreros and serapes decorated the walls of the small, cozy restaurant. To Chase's relief, the hostess showed them to a corner booth away from a noisy family in the center of the room. A quiet dinner with a handsome man hadn't proven such a bad idea...so far.

Her brain kept issuing reminders that beyond tonight's dinner, she wasn't interested in him. Still, there was a draw to his handsome exterior. Obviously, as Mr. Wonderful munched on chips and salsa, he didn't feel the same attraction.

She whisked away feelings of remorse and dipped one of her own chips in the milder salsa. She struggled to concentrate on something other than the way Blaine's blue shirt accentuated his tanned face and complimented his eyes, but her efforts failed.

The ceiling fan stirred a chill breeze and caused the stubby candle in the middle of the table to flicker. Thankful for her sweater, Chase shrugged her shoulders upward, hiding in the warmth. She studied the bill of fare. A single lock of her hair danced in time with the swirling blades overhead; she nonchalantly smoothed it back into place and peered over the menu at Blaine. "Why in the world do they need a fan at this time of year?"

"To keep the air circulating, I suppose. Are you cold?"

Her heart quickened. Hopefully he didn't think she hinted for him to come to her side of the table and put a warming arm around her.

He buried his gaze in his menu again. "Try a little of their hot sauce. That'll warm you up."

If she had expected him to spring to her defense, his response dashed her hopes. But then, had she really expected anything more from him?

She focused on her menu again. "So what do you recommend?"

"Everything," he said between crunches.

"It all looks so good, I don't know what to order." She licked her lips. Did she mean what was on the menu or across from her? Damn that candlelight flickering in his sensuous eyes.

Down girl, it's clear he's not interested in you. Her mind flashed the warning in bright neon.

After the waitress took their order, Blaine propped his chin on his palm. "So, what made you decide to do investigations?"

The clear blue of his eyes matched the sky in the picture painted on the wall behind him. She swallowed, forcing herself to focus on his question.

"Television, I guess. I watched private investigator shows when I was younger and decided I always wanted to be like Barnaby Jones when I grew up."

Blaine's throaty laugh raised goose bumps on her arms. "I'm sure glad you grew up a lot better looking than Barnaby." His comment surprised her more than words could express. Of course, he compared her to an old man with white hair, but he'd given her some sort of compliment...hadn't he?

"Thanks." She squirmed in her seat. God, was she doing something stupid like batting her eyelashes at him?

"Do you miss Sacramento?" His change of topic was the respite she needed.

"Not really. I was ready for something new, although I do miss shopping trips to Old Sac."

"I was there once. It's quite a place, isn't it? I went to a convention about three years ago and dined on the Delta Queen. Lots of nice little shops, but I'm not into that." He rolled his eyes

"What are you into?" Was she being too forward?

"Work. I love my job."

She wanted to ask about his personal life, but that would make her seem too interested in him. Keep it professional, she reminded herself. "Why are you looking at Damien Sloan?"

"Let's just say he's under scrutiny because of his previous employer."

"Genospec?" She leaned against the back of the booth. She'd done her homework.

"Never heard of that place. Why?"

"That's the last employer he listed on his application."

"How about Fossett Labs?"

She shook her head. "I don't recall seeing that listed."

"Have you made any reference calls on Mr. Sloan?"

"Not yet. I was about to do that when you came into my office today."

He chuckled. "Do you always make phone calls

from under your desk?"

An image of her exposed derriere flashed through her mind. "Very funny. Let's just stick to the facts, shall we detective?"

"Gee, you even sound like Barnaby Jones." Blaine flashed a teasing grin. "The facts...according to our records, Damien Sloan's last place of employment was Fossett Labs. He ticked off a senior researcher and got fired. After they collected his keys and sent him packing, someone discovered a bunch of missing files. Seems Mr. Sloan engaged in illegal business practices on his off time."

"Goodness, what was he doing?" She leaned in.

"Since we are speaking one professional to another, I suppose I can share information...especially since I'm going to need your help."

The waitress placed their orders on the table, but Chase was much too engrossed in what Blaine was about to share. "My help?" She toyed with her fork. "Just exactly what am I supposed to do?"

"Mr. Sloan was involved in fertility studies at Fossett and decided to do a little freelancing on the side. The research company paid woman to donate ovum for study, and rather than doing what he was hired for, Sloan pilfered through the files, contacted perspective donors and arranged to harvest their donations at on off-site location."

"How in the world did he get women to

participate?"

"He had no intention of using the eggs for research. He cleverly arranged to work off-hours and, instead, sold the stolen eggs to less-then-reputable fertility clinics and pocketed the money. By luring only an occasional victim off site, he went unnoticed for a long time because the unsuspecting women simply believed they were doing what they had been paid to do."

Chase's mouth gaped. "He sold their eggs without consent?"

Blaine took a sip of water. "Yep."

"How did you find out?"

"One of the donors got suspicious when he asked her to come to a deserted office on a Saturday. Even though he'd dressed in doctor's garb, he didn't have a female assistant, and that sent up a red flag. The woman feigned illness and called off the procedure, but by the time we followed up on her complaint, the company had already sent him packing."

"Thank God! I can't believe other women didn't think something was strange. Of all the nerve! This guy must be some piece of work."

Blaine's forehead filled with lines. "This whole thing about donating eggs seems strange to me, but...."

"There's a great big difference between

donating your eggs for study as opposed to having them used to impregnate someone. For heaven's sake, he was creating children without the real mothers' knowledge. That gives me the creeps."

"When you look at his crime like that, he seems even worse than I thought. Just think of all the women who might run into a child someday that could belong to her." He visibly shuddered.

Chase managed a bite of her enchilada and swallowed. "How did you find out Sloan applied with us?"

"We assumed he'd continue with his moneymaking scheme, so we've been checking all genetic firms."

"So, what can I do to help?"

"I need you to hire him."

She swallowed hard and stared at Blake. "You what? You're kidding, aren't you? Why would I do that after what you've told me?"

"You aren't supposed to know anything, remember? Besides, if you hire him, we can catch him in the act. I'm pretty sure he has no idea the police are onto his little scheme yet."

He paused a moment. "But...that's not the only thing I need from you...."

"What?" She crinkled her brow. "I don't like the way you said that."

"Has Sloan ever seen you?"

"No." Even she noticed the dubious edge to her voice. "Why?"

"Because you're on our new list of donors."

Chase stared at him in wide-eyed amazement. "Me?"

"It's the only way to catch him in the act. Are you certain he's never seen you before?"

"I'm positive...and I'm almost afraid to ask, but what do you expect me to do?"

Blaine nudged his plate aside and rested his arms on the table. "We've made up bogus files under assorted names and will plant them where he'll have easy access. No matter which file he picks, you'll be the donor whose contact info is inside."

"And then?" Chase had a bad feeling about the whole idea.

"Then you'll be the one who meets up with him. You'll give us the perfect opportunity to nab the creep while he's committing the crime."

Her head teetered from side-to-side. "Oh, meet up with him. Is that all?" Sarcasm laced her voice.

"You don't need to worry. You'll be under constant surveillance and in no danger whatsoever."

"There's just one tiny problem."

His brow arched. "What?"

"How am I supposed to hire him without been seen? Besides conducting the background investigation and recommending applicants for interview, I'm also the person who notifies applicants of their acceptance. One of my main responsibilities is greeting the new employees, having them fill out the required paperwork, and making sure all their questions get answered. I can't very well do that and be your pawn, too."

Blaine thought a moment. "That does present a problem. I'll speak to your supervisor and have someone step in and take your place until we collar Sloan."

Chase leaned her head back and stared at the ceiling. "Why me, oh Lord?"

Blaine touched her arm. "Don't worry. Everything will be fine, I promise."

She still felt the warmth of his fingers when he withdrew them. Why did he have to be so darn good-looking?

She took a long, cleansing breath. "How can you be so sure? Say Mr. Sloan contacts me and asks me to meet him in some sleazy warehouse. Won't he be suspicious if I come with company?"

"You won't."

"Well, I'm certainly not going by myself."

"Trust me, I won't let anything happen...and he doesn't meet women in sleazy warehouses. He usually uses a clinic of some sort."

"And that's supposed to make me feel better?"

"I have everything under control. You won't be

alone, and you don't have to worry. Also, I might suggest if you don't already know the process for egg collecting, or whatever it's called, you might want to read up on the topic. I'm sure your company has the appropriate literature."

She narrowed her eyes. How dare he intimate she was ignorant about her own body? She turned a burning stare on him. "I'm quite certain I know everything I need to know. After all, I've been a woman for quite some time now. I'll bet I've had more experience with the female fertility process than you, and harvesting is the term you were looking for." Annoyance showed in her smug response.

If she wasn't mistaken, his face turned red. "I...I'm afraid you misunderstood," he stuttered. "I only wanted to make sure you were prepared for any questions Sloan might ask you. I'm sorry if you're offended."

Why was she acting so defensive? What was it about Blaine Logan that attracted her one-minute and pissed her off the next? He'd really done nothing wrong.

"No, I'm sorry," she insisted. "I overreacted. Must be nerves."

"Oh please, don't be nervous. Like I said, I'll watch over you. I sure don't want anything to happen...especially since we've just met."

His voice faded to a whisper at the end.

She tilted on ear toward him. "What did you say?"

"I said I wouldn't let anything happen to you." He raised his voice to be heard.

"Oh, I thought I heard something more." A wave of disappointment passed through her but she hoped it didn't show. Although she had no appetite, she took a bite of her chilled refried beans and forced a swallow. "We'd better eat before our food gets totally cold...or before I try to talk myself out of this fiasco you've put together."

***

Blaine stopped the car in front of Chase's apartment and turned off the ignition. He shifted around in his seat so he faced her. "Chase, I really enjoyed your company tonight. I hope we can do this again, but not for business reasons."

Her heart hitched. Was he really asking her out again? Talk about someone hard to figure out. He baffled her.

"I'd really like that." She answered before her brain engaged.

"Me, too, but in the meantime, we'll be spending lots of time together on the job. I'll contact your supervisor first thing tomorrow and request Sloan be offered a position, then I'll bring over the bogus files. Once we have them within his reach, you'll have to make yourself scarce. Here's a cell phone programmed with the number Sloan will use to contact you. We've put a bug on the line so that everything discussed will be recorded."

Chase took the phone and giggled. "I guess I won't be calling any of those 1-900 dating lines then." She tucked the phone in her purse.

He grasped her hand. "I can't believe you'd ever need to call a dating service. I'd much rather you call me instead."

The breath she was about to take halted in her throat, and she peered into those luscious blue eyes again. The evening wasn't turning out as she'd expected.

"You know," she found her voice. "You really are a hard person to read. I had a whole different opinion of you before this evening."

"I hope if I made a bad impression earlier, I was able to change it to a positive opinion." He turned on the ignition and checked the clock on the dash. He avoided making eye contact, almost as if he feared what she might say. She said nothing.

The interior light shone dimly overhead. "It's getting late. I'd best walk you to your door. We have a lot to do tomorrow."

She remained in her seat, fingers trembling, as he walked around the car and helped her out. The warmth of his hand stilled her nervousness.

Blaine continued to grasp her palm as they walked to the entry of her apartment complex. She placed her key in the lock, but hesitated before turning it and looked back at him. "Thanks for a great evening. I had a wonderful time." She covered her mouth to hide the giggle brewing in her throat. "I really hope we're still friends when the sting is all over...that is what you call it, isn't it?"

"Yep, it's a sting, and I have no doubt we might grow even closer." Even in the moonlight, his straight pearly teeth sparkled behind his dazzling smile. Couldn't he have at least one visible imperfection?

His face drew closer to hers, and warm breath caressed her face. "Just in case, I'm wrong, would you mind if I kiss you?"

What could one kiss hurt? She titled her chin up, slowly closed her eyes and leaned in. Blaine's lips touched hers, softly at first, but as he turned her to face him and gathered her into an ample embrace, his kiss became more than just a goodnight peck. His tongue flicked against her mouth, seeking entrance.

Her keys jingled, swinging in the lock as both her arms locked around his neck. One hand clung to his shoulder, while the other splayed fingers through his hair. She parted her lips, allowing him to deepen the kiss. Her knees turned to jelly and she sagged against him. Heat traveled through her body, gathering at the juncture between her thighs. Far too many nights had passed since she'd had sex. His manhood hardened against her. She stifled a gasp.

Breathless and craving more of Blaine's touch, Chase ignored the warning bells in her head.

"I'd better stop while I can." Blaine whispered against her hair, then held her at arm's length. "You're quite the kisser." He stepped back and smoothed his pants, attempting to hide his erection, but peered up at her. "Goodnight, Ms. Holmes. I'll see you tomorrow, bright and early.

Giddy from this kiss, all Chase could do was smile and nod. He walked back to his car, while she stood speechless, supporting herself against the stucco wall. When he finally drove away, she took a deep breath, opened her apartment, felt inside for the light switch, and turned it on. She closed and locked the door behind her and let the impact of what had happened between them sink in. With her keys in one hand and her shoulder bag still draped in place, she outlined her lips, recalling the passionate kiss she'd just shared. Sanity snapped her back to reality as soon as her thoughts wandered too far. What had she been thinking? Blaine was a police detective. She couldn't get involved with him.

After switching off the light, she found her way to the bedroom, following the moonbeam path filtering through her window. She undressed, wondering what the feel of his hands on her body would stir—to touch him—taste him.

Naked, she walked into the bathroom and turned on the shower. After the water warmed, she stepped inside and let the comforting liquid pelt her sore muscles. Rivulets running between her breasts and drizzling down her stomach brought forth unwanted visions of Blaine's fingers caressing her skin.

Attempting to purge the thoughts from her mind, she stood beneath the showerhead and turned her face upward. Perhaps the warm, pelting stream would numb her brain and still her imagination.

While water cascaded over her, she covered her loofah with bath soap and ran her hand back and forth over the slime until she created a heap of bubbly lather. Determined to wash the man out of her system, she massaged her neck, chest, and then dipping lower to wash the part of her body that throbbed for pent-up release.

Her attempts failed. Even after shampooing her hair, Blaine filled her every thought. She fought images of his face, body, eyes and lips...those full lips begging to be kissed, and those eyes that enticed her to pursue her urges with his hard and fit body. Was there no way to rid her mind of him?

Hanging her sodden head, she turned her back to the shower and let the water drum against her shoulders. Maybe, just maybe, relaxation would come.

****

Blaine showered and donned a pair of well-worn flannel pajama bottoms. He wandered into the living room and turned on the television. Thoughts of Chase jumbled his mind. He hadn't gone to Norwell Industries looking for a love connection, but there was something about her he couldn't resist...or forget.

Maybe it was the way her hair framed her angelic face, or perhaps her spunky personality and how she called him on his bullshit answers. Either way, he surprised himself when he asked her out. Had he surprised her, too?

Most likely he had since he detected a trace of hesitation on her part during their dinner date—a wall she'd put up between them. But, as the evening progressed, her attitude appeared to have changed. Of course, he relaxed and allowed himself to enjoy their time together.

He was well aware he'd been accused of being an asshole more than once. The fine line between arrogance and confidence blurred when it came to him, but for a chance with the sweet Ms. Holmes, he would definitely try to make some changes.

Blaine flipped through channels, but his thoughts drifted to his promise to keep Chase safe during their joint effort to jail Damien Sloan. Putting anyone into jeopardy came with risks, but Blaine meant what he said. Was he up to the challenge though? Should he cancel the whole stakeout thing and find another way? Sloan had won the trust of so many women; why would his meeting with Chase be different? His confidence waning, Blaine considered calling her to admit there might be more danger involved than he'd indicated.

He held the phone in his hand, but didn't dial. He couldn't let her think he'd lied about keeping her safe—that he wasn't a man of his word. He'd just have to show her he was. Besides, working together gave him the opportunity to get to know her better—in every sense. He put the phone away, recalling what a good kisser she was.

Images of teasing the rosebud tips of her breasts and exploring the enticing vee just below her navel turned his cock rock hard. His fantasy continued as he squirmed in discomfort. First, he'd stir her into a frenzied passion then give her the ride of her life on his stallion of love.

"Yuck! How corny can you be Blaine?" He released the erection he held in his hand while contorting his face into a disgusted look. "No wonder people think you're an asshole."

The air became uncomfortably warm. Rising, he went to the fridge for a cold beer. A smile tugged at his lips as he bent to retrieve the bottle, replaying the image of Chase's pleasing backside greeting him when he'd first entered her office. The girl certainly made a great first impression.

****

Chase arrived at her desk early to be sure everything was in perfect order for whomever would be assuming her duties during her 'donor' stint and to have a chance to review Damien Sloan's folder one more time.

The 'sting' brought Blaine to mind, along with his goodnight kiss. The papers in front of her blurred as her thoughts drifted to places more interesting than the work she needed to finish. Images of a naked Blaine, willing and anxious to bed her etched themselves into her brain, but the opening door startled her. She sat bolt upright, her mind wiped clear of her inappropriate thoughts...at least inappropriate for the workplace.

Blaine strode in, carrying an attaché case. The enticing aroma of his aftershave wafted across her desk and scented the air. Chase steeled herself against returning to 'dreamland.' "Good morning, detective." She used her most professional voice.

"Mornin' yourself, pretty lady. Are you ready to get started?"

Now it was pretty lady? Why was he being so nice? Yesterday, his cocky attitude made it easy to be pissed at him, now when she'd resolved to keep her distance, he wasn't playing fair.

She covered a fake yawn. "I suppose I am. I got an email from my supervisor this morning telling me to cooperate with the Police Department in every way possible."

"*Every* way?" His emphasis on 'every' showed a trace of his smugness.

"You know what I mean."

Blaine sat, opened his briefcase and revealed several different colored file folders. He scooped them up and handed them across to her. "Here are your new identities. Each file has a different name but the same contact number—the cell phone I gave you last night. There are two sets."

She nodded. "So any folder Damien Sloan pulls will bring him to me?"

"Right." Blaine closed his case and glanced at his wristwatch. "Mr. Sloan should be receiving a phone call from your supervisor right about now, telling him he has the job."

"So, what do I do now?"

"After you give your boss one set of folders so they can be planted where Sloan will have easy access, make yourself scarce."

"And go where?"

"You said you needed time to unpack and get settled; here's your chance. Go home and keep busy until Sloan calls you."

"You're kidding, right?"

"Nope. You can't hang around here and risk being seen until he arranges a meeting with you. Sounds pretty cushy to me, especially when you're being paid for your time. Grab your stuff. I'll give you a ride home."

Chase's car was parked in the company lot. His offer tempted her to leave her vehicle and take him up on the ride, but her sense of reasoning prevailed. How would she get back later? Besides, she kept the 'distance' warning flashing in her head. After all, he was a policeman. Holding him at arm's length proved much more difficult than she ever imagined.

"Thanks for the offer, but I have my own car."

He showed a brief scowl. "Okay, fine. As much as I'd love to come over and help you unpack, Sloan isn't my only case."

"I understand." She held her hands like an uneven scale. "Unpacking versus detecting...hmm, I'd say unpacking takes a backseat."

Blaine stood, making everything in the office appear smaller. A slight dimple dotted his cheek when he smiled. "At least let me walk you to your car." He walked around the desk. "We can drop the extra folders off on the way."

"That really isn't necessary." Her internal alarm bell conflicted with her desire to jump into his arms.

She leaned her chair back, putting distance between them.

"I insist."

Confused by her duplicate emotions, she took his offered hand and rose. "How will I know if the call is from Mr. Sloan?" Changing the subject might help.

"Oh…" He released her hand and reached inside his breast pocket. "I almost forgot a really important element. Here's a list of the names appearing on the files. It should be a big help."

She accepted a tablet filled with his scrawl. "If I can read them, it's for sure they'll come in handy. Otherwise I'd just think someone had reached a wrong number."

Blaine opened the door and gestured. "After you." He dropped one gorgeous eye in a wink. "Sorry I forgot the list and that my penmanship doesn't pass muster. I'm a detective not a Rhode's scholar."

She grabbed the extra set of folders. "I think I may be able to qualify for that honor. I've done my homework on donors and I'm ready." She preceded him into the hallway and walked with him to the secretary's desk outside her boss' office. After a brief explanation, she deposited the files. She stuffed her hands in her pocket so he wouldn't be tempted to hold one.

The long corridor was deserted, and during the lull in their conversation, she focused on the rustling noise his pants made with each step he took. She hustled to keep pace with his long stride.

Obviously, from his physique, he worked out. Warning bells, again!

The hallway was overly warm. Where was the air? What was really beneath those slacks? She rolled her eyes at such immature thinking. Imagining body parts? That was something a love-starved teenager might do. She squared her shoulders, demanding more maturity from herself and stared at the floor, counting the floor tiles between her and the door.

From the corner of her eye, she caught Blaine staring at her.

She jerked her head up and faced him. "What?"

Concern etched his handsome face. "Are you sure you're okay with this operation?"

She shrugged. "I guess. Why?"

"I just wanted to make sure. You seem very distant."

At the exit, he stopped and turned to her. "You really don't have to worry. I won't let anything happen to you. I plan to get to know you better."

Her cheeks grew even warmer. Lord, was he really interested in her? The affection showing deep in his eyes led her to believe he was. And wasn't that the same phrase he mumbled at the restaurant last night—or something close?

Blaine turned and opened the door. "Where's

your car?"

She pointed. "The red Honda."

She clicked the alarm button on her keys and unlocked the doors. Now she wished she had accepted his offer of a ride home. Despite every alarm in her body sounding, she didn't want to leave him. Again, the awkward silence cried for her to speak. "Here we are. Thanks for coming along for the walk." She fought the urge to fling her arms around his neck and seek another kiss, but that wouldn't be appropriate.

Like a true gentleman, he opened her door and stood holding the handle while she slid behind the wheel. Before she could fire the ignition, he bent, leaned inside, and planted a soft kiss on her lips. The shock left her with eyes closed and mouth agape. Her heart raced.

"Just hang out at home until Sloan phones. By the way, would you mind if I call you later?"

She opened her eyes slowly and took a deep breath. "Of course I don't mind. I'll be at home, unpacking like a good girl." Despite her brain denying his request and trying to keep her at a safe distance, her mouth reacted from her heart.

He backed away, leaving room to close the door. "I'll talk to you later then." Her heart fluttered as the latch clicked. She hated that his eyes sparkled when he smiled...the way her resolve crumbled every time he looked at her. He was long gone by the time she'd recovered enough to start the engine.

****

A whole week passed and Chase still hadn't heard from Damien Sloan. She and Blaine has spent hours talking on the phone, mostly under the guise of discussing the case, but by the end of each conversation she grew more attached. So much for holding him at bay.

Blaine has strong family ties to three younger brothers and aging parents. Familiarity with the city came natural to him since this was where he'd grown up. He possessed good morals; she respected that. Too bad he'd decided to follow a crime-stopping career. Other than his profession, he was perfect—too perfect.

Chase curled up in her chair with a pamphlet and reached to turn on the reading lamp. If only Blaine could see her now, he'd wonder why she'd been on her high horse about knowing all about her body.

After giving his suggestion further thought, she'd decided perhaps she didn't know everything she needed to know about pre and post-ovulation. In fact, she knew very little. She began reading aloud from *The Menstrual Cycle and Ovulation Prediction* brochure she'd gotten from the lab.

"A woman's fertile period during her menstrual cycle, on average, lasts about nine days—seven before ovulation (the release of the egg), the day of ovulation, and the day after. Following this period, the chances of conception decreased quickly as the egg has a short life-span of about twenty-four hours for fertilization."

She lowered the pamphlet. "Hmm, that might be important if I tried to get pregnant or wanted to avoid it."

Chase placed the reading material aside. "Bring it on, Sloan, I'm ready for ya."

She walked into the kitchen and stared out the window above the sink. Claustrophobia closed in and her anxiety level heightened. How much longer did she have to sit and wait for something to happen?

To detract herself from worrying, she surveyed her kitchen and took pride in her productivity. All the boxes had been unpacked and everything put away. The room was neat as a pin and she planned for it to stay that way…of course, her plans didn't always pan out, but her intentions were great. Mom would be so proud, especially if Chase's old habits didn't die as hard as people claimed.

A glance at the clock explained the rumble in Chase's stomach. Noon. The moment she opened the fridge, the phone rang. Her heart pounded so hard she forgot her grumbling tummy. She closed the door and made for the phone.

The list of names from Blaine lay next to the phone. She picked it up with trembling hands and clicked the answer button on the cell.

"Hello, Mrs. Teller?"

Chase quickly scanned the list: Opperman, Pope, Teller…Sharon Teller to be exact. "Yes, this is she."

"This is Dr. Damien Sloan from Norwell Genetic Industries. I have your donor information, and I'd like to set up an appointment during your next ovulation period. Do you have any idea when that might be?"

The ugliness of his picture didn't match the timbre of his voice. She shivered, knowing the schemer with whom she dealt.

"This must be your lucky day." She tried to keep a steady voice as she formulated a convincing lie. "I've been taking my temperature and using the test kit I was given, and I'm in my most fertile time this week." She cradled the cordless phone in the crook of her neck and wrung nervous hands while she paced.

"You're right. This is my lucky day, isn't it? I didn't expect we would meet quite so soon." His chuckle sounded devious as she paired it with the evil grin in his photo, and caused her to grimace. Luckily he couldn't see her face, and she so prayed the wiretap worked and Blaine listened in.

"So," Sloan cut the silence. "Which day this week would be good for you to meet with me? I'll be collecting your ovum personally."

She shivered at the thought of his hands

coming near her. "I...I'm free tomorrow afternoon." After a breath, she forced herself to respond, even though she wanted to hang up and forget he'd ever called. What had she agreed to do?

"Fine. The address is 1443 Willow Place, Suite A, on the south side of town. Are you familiar with the area?"

"I'm sure I can find it." She played along while trying to pose questions a normal donor would. "Is that where NGI is located?"

"Oh, no." He answered without a hitch. "We don't do collection at the research lab. We maintain separate facilities for that. Shall we plan on around two o'clock?"

The man was smooth, she'd give him that.

"That should work. Is there anything special I should do or bring?"

"Just wear something comfortable, and don't worry."

Sure thing. She'd be meeting with a criminal mind who did evil things to make money, but don't worry...small order. "I'll see you then, Dr. Sloan." She responded with forced politeness although she wanted to throw in 'creep' in place of his name. With her hand shaking and a palm soaked with perspiration, she hung up the phone and sat down in the chair next to her. She took deep breaths and reminded herself to remain calm. She'd just put a sting in place. Who wouldn't be calm after that? She chuckled.

The phone rang again and she nearly jumped out of her skin. "You okay?" The husky voice when she answered slowed her racing pulse.

"Yeah, just a little nervous. Did you hear? That was pretty intense."

"I heard. Sloan's quite the smooth talker. Say...are you busy tonight?"

"Nope."

"Mind if I drop by so we can discuss tomorrow's plan? We don't have much time to get you ready."

"I'll be here."

She hung up, visions of Dr. Sloan replaced by Blaine's piercing, beautiful blue eyes...until she reminded herself to keep her mind on business. She'd already lost someone she loved dearly, and she certainly didn't want to relive the pain of her father's death. Blaine's job put him in harm's way every day, and why she'd agreed to be part of his plan stymied her. It had to be those eyes.

****

Chase struggled to maintain some semblance of space between her body and Blaine's. His arm rested along the back of the sofa, and even though she yearned to nestle against him, her inner self held her steady. The same instructions kept ringing in her mind:

treat tonight like a tennis match and play only one side of the net. Through her inner turmoil, she somehow managed to pay attention for her own safety. Sloan was a dangerous man and she planned on surviving their meeting.

With the plan in place and completely spelled out, Blaine turned to Chase. "Okay, you know where you need to go. Show up on time, follow Sloan's instructions and we'll bust in and nab him."

"Sounds so simple. I'll meet with Sloan but before he even touches me, you'll ride in and rescue me." Her romantic image of a knight on a white horse slipped into her speech. Why wouldn't she get out of the romance mode? She inched a little in the opposite direction to increase the distance between them.

Blaine snared her back and pulled her into an embrace. "Why are you being so stand-offish?"

"I...I'm not." She lied, surprised he'd noticed.

"Yeah, well I think you have something besides Sloan on your mind."

"It's nothing, really." She struggled to get away.

He held her tight. "I'm not going to let go until you tell me, so...."

Chase exhaled and risked gazing into his beautiful blue eyes. Her heart fluttered. "Okay, here's the rub. I really like you Blaine...."

"But?"

"But, my father was a police captain, killed

while doing his job. My mother worried herself sick about him every day, and then her worst nightmare came true. I can't risk getting involved with someone who might end up the same way after seeing what she went through." Tears misted Chase's eyes.

Blaine's brows arched. "I had no idea. I'm sorry about your dad, Chase, but you can't let that color your feelings. Every job is dangerous." He pulled her closer. "Life gives us no guarantee, and not every police office is gonna die in the line-of-duty. I'm just as likely to get killed crossing the street or having a heart attack. If I thought otherwise, I'd never go to work again."

Chase stopped resisting and pressed her cheek against his chest. "What you say makes perfect sense, but I guess I'm just not over losing him."

Blaine kissed the top of her head. "All I ask is that you give *us* a chance. I'm not asking for a commitment, just wanting to see where our 'relationship' goes.

Her mind still objected but her body yearned for him. Her nipples tingled, and then pebbled and her breathing grew heavy with want. Did she dare let down her guard? What if she really fell for him? What if....?

She turned doubting eyes up, but nodded. What could happen if she followed her heart? Raising her head closer to his face, she silently begged for a kiss.

Blaine wiped the tears from her cheeks with a softness she didn't expect, then bent to capture her trembling lips.

She twined an arm around his neck and pulled him closer, wanting to savor his passion. One hand unbuttoned his shirt then moved to his belt buckle. The sound of his zipper sliced the silence, but stirred Chase's excitement. She dipped her hand inside the band of his underwear and...

Blaine's ringing phone dashed the moment.

****

By noon, Chase had practically worn a trench in the worn living room carpet with her pacing. Her second thoughts about being a participant in a sting, let alone being the key player, were a little late in coming.

She had to be at 1443 Willow Place, Suite A by two o'clock, and if she bowed out now, the entire plan would be ruined. Besides, Blaine assured her she'd be safe as a baby.

Thoughts of last night stopped her dead in her tracks. Blaine's kiss was delicious, but her body craved more than just oral gratification. Nonetheless, duty had summoned, and he left.

She giggled at memories of his dishevelment

after he took that annoying phone call. He'd stood, zipped his pants, buttoned his shirt back and tucked in the tails, all the while looking like a little boy who didn't get his desert. His attempts to conceal the evidence of his lust were futile, and she hoped he hadn't noticed her lusting stares. Had she drooled?

She snapped back to reality. Where were all these X-rated thoughts coming from? She'd never been a sex fiend, although she did enjoy a good screw. Why was climbing into bed with Blaine dominating her every thought these days? A deep, cleaning breath slowed her heart and allowed her reasoning mind to function again.

If what she felt was sexual frustration, relief would have to wait for a more appropriate time. She had a job to do...a very important one. Still, a smile tugged at her lips...satisfaction in knowing Blaine obviously wanted her just as much.

Realizing she hadn't eaten, Chase sat at the table and forced down a blueberry muffin. Her coffee had already turned cold but helped wash down her skimpy lunch. The last thing she wanted was a growling stomach when she met Dr. Sloan. She already had an upset one.

The cell phone Blaine gave her rang. She almost jumped out of her chair, but relaxed at the thought that perhaps Sloan was calling to cancel. Wouldn't that be grand?

"Chase, it's me." Blaine's voice greeted her.

She sighed. "I thought you might be the doctor."

"Disappointed?"

"No! I mean yes. I'm glad you called, but I sort of wish you were Sloan telling me you have the flu or something worse."

Blaine's chuckle made her breath hitch. "I just called to remind you not to worry. Everything will be fine."

"From your lips to God's ear."

Blaine chuckled again. "Just remember, I'll be there. Okay?"

"I know." She offered up confidence, but doubt still niggled at her.

****

Chase checked her watch as soon as she hung up. Twelve-thirty. A tension headache loomed to add misery to her churning stomach, but she didn't have time to whine. She hadn't yet grown familiar with the town, but Blaine had provided a map to the clinic to gauge the travel-time needed. By her estimation, she still had a little time to kill.

Kill...that was a bad choice of words to come to mind.

The novel she'd been reading lay on the coffee

table. She tucked her phone in her purse, curled up in her well-worn easy chair, and returned to the page she'd marked.

The words on the page ran together. She couldn't concentrate, besides this wasn't a good time to concentrate on romance. Although fiction, the story stimulated sexual thoughts about Blaine she certainly shouldn't be having…at least not now. She slapped the book closed and glanced at her wristwatch again. Five whole minutes had passed.

Her phone rang again. She fished it out of her purse.

"Hello."

"Dr. Sloan here."

"Oh, Doctor, I was just getting ready to leave for our appointment." The hair on her arms stood on end.

"Then I'm glad I caught you. I need to make a last minute change."

Oh please cancel…please, her brain begged.

The cell phone started to beep, begging for a recharge. She stifled a gasp at the realization Blaine hadn't given her the cord. Already something had gone wrong. Maybe there was something to her feelings of dread.

She had to act fast before the cell went dead completely. "Dr. Sloan, can you give me your number so I can call you back? My phone is fading fast."

She lost the connection as she jotted down the last digit.

Her pulse raced as she grabbed the landline. Blaine wouldn't be able to hear her conversation. Questions muddled her mind, but she didn't want to make Sloan suspicious. She dialed his number.

"I'm really sorry about that," she said when he answered.

"No problem. I called because I need to change the address where we'll meet."

Her shoulders tensed. "Why?"

"Nothing to fret about, my dear. There was a small fire in the complex this morning, and the smoke is still fairly thick. I've arranged to use another doctor's office."

Was he lying? Why would he change the location at the last minute? Oh, God, what should she do?

Recalling her obligation, she copied down the new directions. "I'll see you there." Her stomach churned even more.

She clutched the phone so tightly her knuckles turned white, and she held it that way until the ended call alarm started screaming. She hung up to still the noise, trying to chart her next move.

She'd call Blaine and tell him about the address change...but she didn't have his personal number. Was this a 911 emergency? She doubted the dispatcher would see it that way, so she pulled out the telephone book and check for the local PD number then dialed. After listening to menu selections and following the required steps, she finally reached a live person.

"Detective Blaine Logan, please." Did her voice sound as frantic as she felt?

The woman put her on hold. Chase drummed her fingers on the table until she realized where the noise came from. The rat-a-tat ended, replaced by the echo of rapid breathing very similar to that produced by someone who'd just run a marathon.

The line clicked and startled her. "Detective Logan is out of the office. Would you like his voicemail?"

"No, that won't help at all." Chase tried to keep the edginess from her voice. After all, it wasn't the woman's fault. "I need to get an urgent message to him right away. Please take down this address and tell him there has been a last minute change of plan. He'll understand, and please have him call Chase Holmes at her home number."

She hung up and checked the time again. Almost one o'clock. Her heart thudded as she paced. Should she stay or go? She'd wait a few more minutes for his call.

At one-twenty, Blaine still hadn't phoned and she couldn't stall any longer. Chase had a decision to make.

Would Blaine be angry if she didn't go? Would she mess up the arrest if she did? At least she could drive there and see, if by some miracle, Blaine got her message. Surely, that wouldn't be dangerous.

She grabbed her purse and directions and then walked out the door.

****

Chase pulled into the parking lot and turned off the ignition with five minutes to spare. She clutched the steering wheel, anticipating what lay ahead.

She scanned the parking lot and surrounding area for Blaine or anyone resembling a police officer but saw no one. She pulled the paper from her pocket on which she'd jotted the new address and stared at it? Which suite was it? Did Blaine get the message?

Don't proceed without knowing Blaine is here, her instincts screamed at her. Go home and call Sloan. Tell him you had a flat tire.

Despite her instincts, stupidity stepped in. You've had training, Chase. You're sort of a private investigator, and Sloan really hasn't hurt anyone. Just see if you can get some information. She grabbed the handle and held the door ajar.

The conversation in her head reminded her of a TV cartoon—the one where a good angel sat on one shoulder and a bad one on the other. "So, do you want to be the first person he hurts?" The good angel asked. "Use your head."

She didn't give the bad angel time to counter. The whole idea seemed stupid now, and she'd gotten some good advice. She closed the door and reached for the ignition key. Someone rapped hard against the window. Her head jerked around to see Sloan's face peering in at her. Fear froze her in place.

He rapped again.

"Caution, caution," her good Angel warned.

Chase inched the glass down just enough to be heard. "Can I help you?"

He pressed his face closer to the opening, sending stale tobacco breath into the car. His leering eyes looked just like his photograph. "You wouldn't happen to be Mrs. Teller, would you?"

His question caught her off guard. "Ah…yes, why yes, I am." She immediately wanted to kick herself for admitting her fake identity when he'd never seen her.

That old familiar smirk crossed his face. "I'm Dr. Damien Sloan. Let me show you to the office."

Chase's gaze caught that her door wasn't locked. Fat lot of good it did to roll the window down just a smidgen. Her first instinct was to reach over and depress the lock button, as she should have already done. And why in the world had she admitted to being Sharon Teller. What a dunce.

Even if she considered trying to lock him out, he'd already opened her door. Her heart pounded like a hammer against an anvil. What did she do now? There was no place to run...not a soul to cry out to.

"Are you feeling all right? You look quite pale."

"Uh...I'm not feeling very well, perhaps we should reschedule the procedure."

"Trust me. The harvesting won't take very long and then you'll be on your way."

On her way? Where...to the morgue? "But I have a terribly upset stomach," she persisted. "Must have been something I ate."

"Let's go inside. I can give you something to make you feel better."

He had a response for everything.

Sloan stepped around the door and offered his hand. Her stomach rolling, she still searched for a convincing excuse to leave. Maybe if she puked on his shoes.

Surrendering to his continued insistence and over-powering presence, Chase foolishly allowed him to help her out of the car.

"Don't forget your keys."

She snared them from the ignition and dangled them for him to see.

The doctor depressed the lock button and closed the door, then he ushered her onto the sidewalk. "Maybe the fresh air will help you feel better." His hand, resting against the small of her back, urged her onward.

She'd only feel better when she saw Blaine.

****

How had she gotten herself into such a mess? Blaine would probably never want to see her again after this…if there was an after.

Inside, Chase relaxed a little upon seeing the suites that adjoined the one Dr. Sloan led her to appeared to be medical offices with people inside. He wouldn't dare try anything if a mere scream brought help running.

He unlocked a nearby door and nudged her inside. The dark and menacing interior changed the moment he flipped on the light and the illumination showed an ordinary doctor's waiting room.

Sliding glass doors decorated with photographs of children and gaily-colored hand drawn pictures separated the reception area from the seats. She found nothing insidious about the place, and relieved for the moment, she placed her keys in her shoulder bag. Of course, chanting in her mind about Blaine's pending arrival didn't hurt.

"Feeling better, Mrs. Teller?" Sloan's voice startled her.

She was slow in responding to her fake name.

"A little." Looks aside, he seemed harmless enough. Still, one hand clutched the top of her bag so tightly, her knuckles ached.

"Come this way, please." He led her through a second door and down a dim corridor.

"You're in dire jeopardy," the good angel warned, as if Chase didn't know.

She had to escape and now, but how?

Chase stopped dead in her tracks. "Really, Dr. Sloan, I think I'd prefer to do this when I'm feeling better. I'm just not up to the procedure today."

He took a step backwards and placed his urging hand in the small of her back again. "Let's step into the exam room and wait a few minutes to see how you feel. I can give you something to help settle your stomach."

She didn't want to 'step inside' but didn't see a way to avoid it. Sloan wasn't being overly threatening, just very insistent.

Maybe if she bolted....

No chance. He stood between her and the door.

"Why don't you have a seat on the table while I get the paperwork started? I'll need your signature before we do proceed."

"O...okay" Her voice sounded shaky, even to her. She stifled a nervous giggle. He was going to do paperwork for an illegal procedure. Yeah, right!

The paper on the examining table crinkled when she perched on the edge. She leaned over and placed her purse on a nearby chair. She had to make him believe she was staying while she figured a quick escape route.

He eyed her hands tightly clasped in her lap. "There's no need to be nervous. This whole thing will be over before you know it." He stepped out and closed the door behind him.

Over? If he meant to make her relax, he'd failed miserably. She took a deep breath. Maybe if she refused to sign…. Oh, where was Blaine when she needed him?

Deciding to make her move, Chase jumped down from the table, grabbed her purse, slung the strap over her shoulder and made for the door. Bad timing! She met Sloan in the doorway. He smelled of medicine and carried a blue paper gown.

"Are you going somewhere?" His tone sounded menacing.

"Y…yes. I've decided against the procedure. As I told you, I'm not feeling at all well."

He laid the gown on the counter, still staying between her and the exit. "I'm very sorry to hear that."

She considered pushing him aside and running, but she retained a calm demeanor, even with her trembling insides. "I'm sorry to put you through all this trouble. Can we please reschedule?"

"Certainly." He moved from the doorway and patted her on the shoulder.

She almost gasped at his sudden agreement.

Opening the door brought a rush of relief. She stopped and looked back at Sloan. "I'll wait to hear from you, and again, I'm very sorry for the inconvenience."

She held her breath and started down the hall.

"Think nothing of it." Sloan's voice sounded from behind her...in a tone far too kind.

She'd almost reached the waiting room door when he grasped her elbow. She gasped in a shocking breath.

"Let me show you out."

She released her pent-up breath and put her hand on the doorknob. She'd made it!

A hand snaked from behind her and covered her mouth and nose with an acrid smelling cloth. A boney arm circled her waist, restraining her and forcing her to inhale the permeating odor. She claw at the gingers covering her face and tried to cry out, but only made a muffled moan.

The lights blurred and the straight lines of the wall turned wavy. When she reached for the door, it seemed to slant away from her. Each blink became slower as she struggled to stay awake. Blaine's name rested on the tip of her tongue, and she yearned to call out to him, but words failed as an unwelcome darkness claimed her.

****

Chase opened her eyes. Her vision blurred and she blinked several times in an attempt to focus. The dots in the ceiling tiles overhead came into view, and the brightness of the fluorescent lights caused her to look away.

Memories rushed back. Her heartbeat notched up and she tried to rise. She failed, discovering her hands restrained.

The drug-induced fog lifted and Chase became aware of her nakedness from the waist down. Her feet were in stirrups beneath a white paper drape. Panic welled in her breast and she scanned the room as best she could. Where was the son-of-a-bitch?

Damien Sloan stood at the counter, holding a long syringe-like tool. Before him, several Petri dishes and a pair of rubber gloves.

She struggled against her bindings, but to no avail as they were secured to the sides of the table. She raised her head and glared at the doctor. "Let me go or I'll scream."

He picked up a white cloth from the counter and turned toward her. "Would you like another dose of chloroform?"

Her head lolled back against the pillow. "Surely, you aren't stupid enough to think you can get away with this, especially after...."

She stopped short of finishing. What was she thinking? Her stupid comments just invited him to kill her. He couldn't leave a witness behind that could testify against him. Oh, Lord, she didn't want to die.

Sloan crossed the room and stood over her. The evil grin on his face as he gently pushed her hair back from her forehead reminded her of a horror movie. "You're absolutely right, my dear. I can't get away with this unless—"

"Please don't kill me. I won't tell anyone if you just let me go."

"I'm afraid I can't do that." He continued to splay her hair away from her face, almost like he was soothing her.

"But why? Is this so important that you have to kill me? Why not just let me go and move onto your next unknowing victim?" She grasped at anything to save herself.

Sloan's evil laugh bounced off the walls. "Just as I thought, *Ms. Holmes,* you already know about me. I suspected as much, so I went through your purse.

"You won't get away with this."

He walked to the counter for the ominous syringe, and then held it in the air like a regal scepter.

"I have someone willing to pay big bucks for your donation. Regardless of how this played out, you were going to be the last. I already figured out I was under investigation, and the money I'm getting from the sale of your eggs is going to take me out of the country. There's no way I'm going to jail."

"Don't be so sure."

He snickered.

Her knees quivered as he insinuated himself between them and pushed them further apart. A cool breeze assaulted her genitals as he raised the drape onto her stomach and left her bottom fully exposed and accessible.

She'd never felt so vulnerable.

While clutching the chloroformed cloth in his hand, he leaned forward and dangled it close to her face. "Just take a deep breath and you won't feel a thing."

Chase jerked her head to the side, trying to escape the noxious odor. "Please don't." The ties cut into her wrists and she wrestled to free herself.

He dropped the cloth on her chest, just below her chin.

"Have it your way. I don't have time to play games. You have to breathe and this will work as well, just not quite as fast."

Chase held her breath. "I'm not going to die, I'm not going to die," she chanted mentally.

His fingers touched her nethermost region; he pushed her legs further apart. She bit her bottom lip and tasted blood. He separated her womanly folds and sought a vital opening. The chloroform turned the room hazy. She swiveled her head to the other side and tipped her jaw up and away, seeking fresh air. Her attempts failed. She grew more and more sleepy.

Something cold and alien slipped inside her. A hot tear rolled down her cheek and into her hair. Fingers of darkness called out to her, and even slammed into the wall so hard the room vibrated.

"What the hell?" Sloan yelled.

Chase batted her eyes, trying to stay awake. She couldn't go to sleep...she had to stay awa—"

****

Her eyes opened to the painful brightness of overhead lights. She squeezed her lids together and then slowly reopened them, averting her gaze from the ceiling.

Seized by panic, she fought against restraints no longer in place. Surprised by the freedom of movement, she raised a trembling hand and touched her brow.

Was she alive?

Fear kept her from glancing down the length of her reclined body. Surely her torment hadn't ended. She couldn't be that fortunate. Had he gone for a weapon? Was it her time to die, after all?"

Her brain screamed for her to escape, but the

drugs still clouded her mind. The room felt chilly. Without looking, she reached down for the drape, but her fingers drifted along a downy blanket. She braved a glance and saw the outline of her feet beneath the covers. Through bleary eyes, she noticed a television suspended in the far corner, and in the distance, heard the murmur of voices.

She shook her head to clear the fog, and then tried to sit, but the room spun. She sagged back onto her pillow, closed her eyes, and sought a moment to sort through everything that had happened.

"Escape…find Blaine…" The good angel still directed her.

A warm hand glanced her brow and startled her. Her eyes opened wide.

"Hi, sleepyhead. Nice to see those beautiful brown eyes of yours."

Misty relief embraced her. She wanted to laugh and cry at the same time.

"Oh, Blaine, you found me." She struggled to speak above a whisper.

"Just in the nick of time. What the heck were you thinking?" He gathered her into his arms. "I was worried sick when I got your message."

"Please don't be mad." She buried her face against his chest.

"I'm not angry. You're safe and that's all that matters. Rest now…it's all over."

****

Chase dozed in and out of a restless sleep, alternating between the nightmare of being tethered to the mad doctor's examination table and the realization she was safe and in the hospital. What a relief it had been to see Blaine's handsome face when she woke.

He'd left earlier with a promise to return, and the anxiousness to talk to him and find out what had happened kept her on edge. Chase had already questioned the nurses on duty and only found out that she'd been unconscious when Blaine brought her to the ER. No one knew the details of her rescue.

"How are you feeling?" He entered with a big smile and a bouquet of red roses.

"Much better, now that I've slept off the affects of that awful chloroform."

He handed the flowers to the nurse and grasped Chase's hand. "You look better. I'm so happy I found you in time. If I had gotten your message just a few minutes later, we wouldn't be having this conversation, and I would have to live with the fact that I lied to you about keeping you safe."

"I'm even more thankful than you are, believe me."

He looked at her beneath raised brows. "So, tell

me, what were you thinking… going there without being sure you'd be protected?"

She pushed the button to elevate the bed. "First, tell me how you found me."

He perched on the edge of the mattress, still holding her hand. "I tried calling your cell phone, but you didn't answer. I tried your home phone, but you didn't answer there either. Finally, dispatch reached me and relayed the new address for your meeting with Sloan. I was already staked out at the other clinic and was so afraid I wouldn't make it across town in time…." His voice crackled with emotion that surprised Chase.

"But you did make it in time." She pulled herself up further, planted a kiss on his lips, but held him at arm's length. "And to think I didn't want to get involved with a policeman. I don't think I'm ever going to feel secure without you around."

He laughed.

Her mind flashed back to her last moments of lucidity…those final moments before she'd drifted into oblivion.

"Wh…what condition was I in when you found me?" Despite being afraid to ask, she dared pose the question.

Blaine leaned his head next to hers on the pillow, propped his feet on the bed and crossed his ankles. "You won't have to worry about Dr. Damien Sloan anymore. Where he's going, he won't be able to hurt you or anyone else for a very long time."

"Blaine?"

"Uh huh."

"Don't avoid my question. Umm...when you found me...what was happening. Did he....?"

Blaine turned to her and winked.

"Dang it, tell me." She pounded his shoulder with her fist.

"Okay, Okay." He held her hand to stop the pummeling. "Remember the first day we met, and you worried I might have seen your charming derriere?"

Her cheeks heated. "How could I forget such a memorable moment?

Without another word, he slipped off the bed and walked to the doorway. He leaned out and looked up and down the hall, then turned and cast an impish grin.

He closed the door, turned off the overhead lights, walked back to the bed and crawled in beside her. "In lieu of all you've been through, I just want to hold you and keep you safe. Nothing happened, and nothing ever will." He cupped her chin and looked deep into her eyes. "In answer to your question,...let's just say I've seen enough of Chastity's charms to make me want to stay around and protect them. Do you mind?"

"Oh, Blaine. Of course I don't mind. You've made me the happiest woman in the world...I'm not

even bothered that you used my given name…and—"
He silenced her with a kiss that curled her toes.

The End

72

FAITH OLIVER
AGE THIRTY-ONE

FAITH

Faith woke with lips feeling bruised from passionate kisses, her breath coming in quick gasps after a voracious bout of sex.

Until last night, her dream lover had only touched and kissed her. She'd never gotten a look at his manhood before, and was awed by the size of it. If anyone considered a penis a weapon, the man was heavily armed.

She pushed herself into a sitting position and rested against the headboard until she was composed. If she smoked, this would be the perfect time for a cigarette. The dream had been the most fantastic so far...and baffling.

Her nameless beau has actually made love to her. Now she knew what she'd been missing. Her nipples remained pebbled beneath her nightshirt, and from something other than cold air for a change. Warm and moist, her inner core still contracted from the thickness of him, and her body quivered with delight. She pinched herself to make sure she was awake. Was this the afterglow she'd heard about?

Still, the overwhelming question haunted her. Who was *he* and why did *he* come to her? Each time she came close to discovering his name, she awoke. Was there a reason? She enjoyed the familiarity of him...the way he comforted her, but she had to figure out this dilemma. She'd seen a lounge performance featuring a hypnotist ages ago. Maybe that was her answer.

She glanced at the clock on the nightstand. Time to get ready for work. She rose from bed and headed for the bathroom.

While the water ran, she stripped off her nightgown and underpants. Catching a glimpse of her reflection, she grimaced at the rolls and flab. Who would ever want to run hand over all those layers? "Hell, even I don't wanna." Living alone led to extended conversations with no one.

Faith stepped into the shower. The warm water soothed her chilled skin, and she covered herself with a generous lather. Her determination to diet grew when she lifted the fold of her abdomen and washed beneath it. Of course, this was the moment every single day she vowed to lose weight, but today she really meant it.

Water drizzled down her upturned face and dripped from the ends of her hair. With eyes closed, she imagined the man in her dreams and the passion he stirred. The dream replayed over in her mind. Her fingers traveled across a man's broad shoulders and down his muscular back. Her palms cupped his taut behind, pulled him closer to take in every inch of his throbbing manhood. He was real; he had to be. A mere vision couldn't instill such feelings.

As hard as she tried to stop the images, she recalled his head between her legs, darting tongue suckling and pleasing her. Her pulse quickened. In her pretense, she delved a foamy finger into her slit and gently massaged until her body quivered with release.

She moved from climax to shampooing her hair, unashamed of having taken care of her own physical needs. A girl had to do what a girl had to do, and that was a fact. She ducked her head beneath the faucet, hoping the water would wash away the sensuous images and unanswered questions...a monumental fail. Could this be how love felt? Maybe, but who in the heck was the man she loved?

Afterwards, Faith wrapped in a beach towel and shimmied a smaller terry cloth version through her sodden locks. Although trying to skirt her reflection upon exiting the bedroom, she cursed her peripheral vision for catching a glimpse of her dimpled behind. Normally, she waited until she was fully clothed to approach any looking glass, and then only focused on things within the scope of instant improvement such as her face and hair. Make-up and well-coiffed tresses made a difference, but anything below the neck was a different story.

Back in the bedroom, light filtered through her floral draperies. Dust motes danced in the air and birds sung in the branches outside. She smiled and caressed her throat where the sensation of warm kisses still lingered.

"Get real, Faith. You've only had a dream." She chastised herself for believing anyone would find her desirable, let alone make love to her. Mornings came with severe disappointment. No matter how much she wanted her lover to be real, he only visited her in sleep.

Straightening the sunflower comforter proved to be a strenuous task. Her breathing grew rapid from the mere exertion, but she managed to finish straightening her bed. People kindly referred to women of her size as "full-figured", but she preferred to see herself as a thin, sexy vixen, trapped in layers of fat—unfair, ugly fat she didn't deserve. Someday she'd find a way to lose weight and be the person she'd always wanted to be, and then she'd seek an explanation for her strange dreams. In the meantime, she perched on the mattress and waited for her breathing to slow. The clock showed she still had plenty of time before her bus departed, so she thought back to her childhood.

Faith, nee Faith Marie Oliver, had been heavy

for as long as she remembered. In grammar school, she'd always been last to be picked for sports activities, and in junior high and high school she always felt out of place because she never got invited to dances or school functions. Boys hadn't wanted anything to do with a fat girl, and even the others of her gender shied away.

She'd had a brilliant idea to surround herself with other 'heavyweights' in an effort to make herself feel better, but she'd outgrown all of them except, Nila, her best bud down the hall. They ran neck and neck in the weight department—teetering around the two-fifty mark.

Now at thirty-one and a working woman, Faith had never been on a real date. It wasn't only high school boys who found excess weight less than desirable; men in general did. She grimaced at the fat ankles and feet protruding from the hem of her nightgown. Yes, after last night, she was through being fat. She wanted to be cherished by someone real and today, she'd initiate a surefire plan to lose weight.

Faith hungered for breakfast, but flashed back to all the fattening meals she'd eaten as a child. Her father died when she was an infant, and every day she wondered how he'd feel about having an overweight daughter. Would he accept and love her?

She enjoyed a good relationship with her mother while she was alive, although they'd struggled to get by on what little money they had. No matter how broke they were, Faith's reward for a good deed had always been something calorie-laden.

Feeling the need for assistance in her resolution, Faith dialed Nila's number. She'd probably be up and getting ready for work by now.

"Hullo." A groggy voice answered.

"Nil, it's me. I need your support."

"Then get a better bra. I still had twenty minutes to sleep before the alarm."

"Stop joking around. We're going on a diet. What say we go out tonight and enjoy a great big salad to celebrate?"

"You had to wake me to ask me that? How do I know what I'll be doing tonight? That's hours away." Her gaping yawn sounded on the phone. "Besides, how do you know I want to be on a diet?"

"Don't tell me you aren't sick of being f...fa...overweight." The "f" word just wouldn't come out. Admitting to being fat was something no one liked. "It's been months since we've done something fun together. I thought if we had one another for support, we might do better. Whadda you say?"

"I might be persuaded to go with you, but I'm not sure about the diet. What's on the menu?"

"Salad...any kind you want."

"That sounds boring." Nila yawned again.

"Well, I'd love the chicken fried steak and

mashed potatoes my mom used to fix, but that's how I got this way. I'm having a salad and turning over a new leaf."

"Yeah, of lettuce. I'll go with you, but I'm not making any promises. I have about as much willpower as a flea."

Faith wished her friend a good day, set a time to meet, and hung up.

The imaginary aroma of the meal she mentioned hung heavy in the air. The loving memories of her mom washed over her, along with her hatred for the brain aneurysm that took her away. Now, Faith had no one but distant cousins she barely knew and Nila.

Eating usually eased her grief, but Faith remained steadfast in her quest. In the past, any trace of trauma sent her into a feeding frenzy, but not today. Laughter and hiding behind a mask of humor would no longer be her coping tool. She was through being the first to make jokes about her weight, thinking once it was mentioned, no one else need comment. Besides, lately finding laugher enough to stifle the pain of having only a dream lover was a chore. How sad to have a special man in one's life who only appeared during sleep.

With the aid of the nightstand, she stood. The amazingly real dreams she'd had for the past three weeks turned her knees weak. Every other morning, she'd awoke to the feel of her nameless lover's hands roaming her body, his lips paying homage to her most feminine parts. But last night….wow! His lovemaking surpassed anything she'd ever experienced.

Looking around the empty room, she chastised herself for believing in the reality of her dreams and lumbered toward the closet. She furrowed her brow when the name 'Joshua' flashed in her mind. Strange, since she didn't know anyone by that name and probably never would.

She shuffled the hangers back and forth, searching for her day's attire. Draping her selected dress on the bed, she eyed the package of panty hose on the bureau. "Why the heck do I even bother," she ranted, while she sat and dried her legs thoroughly.

"Obviously some man decided a woman's legs should be encased in something other than her own skin, and for this idea, we spend mounds of money on something we only wear once because another man made the product so flimsy they don't last." With each ranting word, she scrubbed the towel harder against her ample calves.

She stood and took the package to the bed, scowling at the bold words "queen-size" emblazoned across the front...like it was a royal announcement of pride. She then removed the product gently from its safety sheath.

Despite being careful, she noticed a pull near the waistband when she let the silken material unravel its full length. "Christ, NASA makes paint to withstand the heat of earth's reentry, you'd think they could make nylons to withstand a hangnail."

She wiggled her way into her sheer cocoon, sensing it wasn't going to be a good day. The snag already zipped across her abdomen and still spread.

"Who gives a crap?" She glanced down at the run. "No one looks at me anyhow."

Instead of crawling back into bed to sleep and recapture the wonderful feelings her dream lover brought, she shimmied into her dress. Why was *his* image so real, and why did her most intimate body parts pulse when she thought of *him*? Most of all…where did *he* come from and why? The answers eluded her.

Perching on the edge of the mattress to slip into her shoes, she pondered her make-believe world and the handsome man there who belonged only to her. Would he love her even more if she were thin? Her euphoric thoughts faded with a glance at the clock on her nightstand. Work always trumped romance, and it was time to think of earning a rent-paying wage, but she stole a moment, closed her eyes and visualized her lover's amazing caress.

Nagged by time passing, her reality returned. There was no man in love with her, no thin body, just the same fat, Faith. She tore the pantyhose package to shreds to vent her frustrations. "How can this be? I've dreamt about the same man for weeks, and I can sense him even after I wake. I smell his musky aroma, and he does things...wonderful, exciting things to me. I couldn't write a better novel than the stuff I dream about. "She gazed at the mess she'd made and clenched her teeth. She likened picking up the pieces to salvaging her life. Her resolve grew as she crawled along and cleaned the litter from the floor. No more computer dating sites, no more scanning ads in the newspaper, and certainly no more sitting at home feeling so depressed she ate herself into oblivion. She was through being referred to as queen-sized, full-figured, plus-sized or even a big, beautiful woman. Who came up with those ridiculous descriptions anyhow? Probably a woman who shared her weight issue because Faith had yet to find a man who listed any one of those terms in his ad for female companionship. Even the ugliest of men on the Internet wanted 'firm, fit and toned.'

She'd let her weight define her, others judge her on looks and tolerated snickers people thought she couldn't hear. She couldn't count the number of failed diets in her life, but she'd never felt the determination she possessed this time around. She stood, huffing from exertion and decided to call Nila one more time before leaving for work. She checked her watch and dialed her friend's number. If Faith didn't share her nightly escapades with someone, she'd burst, and Nila was the only person she trusted. Right now, Faith needed assurance she hadn't gone stark-raving mad.

"Okay, Faith," Nila answered. "This had better be important because you got me out of the shower."

"For a minute I thought you had turned psychic, but then I remembered you have caller ID,"

"I'd have known it was you without it. No one else calls me." She gave a hearty laugh. "What's so urgent you needed to call me twice? Let me guess…you decided we're having burgers tonight instead of salad. Nila snickered.

Nila had a great sense of humor, and Faith adored her. Even though their relationship had grown close over the years, Faith never had the courage to ask her friend if she was as happy as she always seemed. How could she be?

"No, we're still having salads…."

Faith hesitated, planning how to approach the reason she'd called. "Uh…you're probably going to think I'm a loon…."

"I already know that for sure. Spit it out, Faith. I don't have time to play guessing games. I'm dripping all over the carpet."

"Have you ever had dreams so vivid they seem real? I'm talking really real."

"Like what?" Nila's voice edged with testiness.

"Oh, anything. For example, have you ever dreamt about someone in particular? Say someone you don't know but swear they actually exist?"

"Is this a joke?"

Silence lingered on Faith's end.

"No, it's no joke." She finally gathered the courage she needed. "I've dreamt about the same man for weeks now, and I feel his touch even after I wake. His aroma lingers on my fingertips, and he does things…."

"Oh for heaven's sake, what kind of things?"

"Sexual things…wonderfully fulfilling things."

"Okay, girlfriend. What have you been eating before you go to bed?"

"I'm serious, Nil. I…he…oh, forget it." Faith sighed. "You're probably right. I need to quit snacking before bedtime. Too much red dye in my diet, but—"

"I'd love to talk about it more, Faith, but I have to run. I can't be late to work. Let's chat more about your dreams over dinner tonight. I can hardly wait to hear about this supposed lover of yours."

Faith hung up, wishing she'd never called. Nila probably thought her friend had lost her blasted mind. Maybe she had.

****

Faith took a break from editing, bookmarking her place in her currently assigned manuscript. Catching grammatical and punctuation errors for Neon

Publishing Agency was a task tedious at times, but extremely difficult when she found herself caught up in the story...like the current steamy romance on her desk, *Taming of the Crew.* The novel featured a lusty college babe who set her sails for the captain of the school's rowing team and screwed all his friends just to make him jealous. Faith imagined being like the heroine and working her wiles on men. If she didn't need to begin an exercise regime, she'd spend her fifteen minutes reading further and hope to gain some pointers. Oh to write a book like that.

As she grabbed her sweater from the coat rack, she giggled. Imagine being an author. What might she write to fit the Erotica genre? The title she edited now was obviously a takeoff on a more serious title. Given her lack of actual sexual knowledge, Faith doubted anyone would be drawn to *Catch Her in the Rye Crisp* or *Fat on a Hot Tin Roof.* Authors had imaginations.

"What the hell?" Her exclamation echoed in the empty hallway. She winced. This talking to herself had to stop. But imagination? She had one. Look at the man she'd dreamed up. She made him erect just by envisioning him with one. Could other heroine's do that? Probably. While Faith dreamed, writers actually put their thoughts into action on paper. She doubted she could be as descriptive since she even had problems talking about her night visions, but living vicariously through romance heroines suddenly wasn't enough.

Faith pounded her fist in the palm of her other hand. Life wasn't fair and if she wanted to truly find a lover, she had to lose weight. Although physical appearance shouldn't keep a man from discovering the great personality inside, Faith buttoned up her sweater and stepped outside. As soon as she finished her walk, she had a plan to put into action.

****

Faith's lap about the block had taken less time than expected. Still she panted like a racehorse. She searched the bookcase behind her desk and withdrew the telephone book. Searching under 'weight loss' she found 'see physicians.'

"Crap, why can't they just put things where they should be?" She thumbed back to the 'P' section and scanned the thousands of headers above the doctors' names. She finally found the column she sought, but so many names. How did one pick?

Closing her eyes, she pointed then peeked. Her finger landed on Dr. Eric Russ. "Hmm, probably as good as any." She put the phone to her ear and dialed, glancing around to make sure no one was in the vicinity...like anyone paid her attention.

"Medical offices, how may I help you?" A woman's voice answered.

"I'd like to make an appointment, please."

****

"Damn diet." Faith clenched her teeth as she revolved in front of the full-length mirror she'd bought for her closet door. The results of the past three weeks and twenty pounds weren't showing up fast enough to suit her. Of course, she hadn't put the weight on overnight, but that fact didn't soothe her eagerness to view a newer, slim body. Her dreams continued, and her lover kept her quite satisfied, but she wanted someone to date…to show off, not someone who couldn't be seen or heard by others.

Nila had already fallen off the wagon. Shortly after their salad dinner and a vow to support one another, she'd gone back to eating calorie-laden foods. When Faith invited her to go for a walk, Nila had laughed. "Not unless you're holding a gun and threatening me."

Dieting wasn't fun, and Faith's determination was tested when she received an invitation to an after-work beer and pizza birthday party. Maybe her decision to pass hadn't been so much willpower, but the desire to hurry home and be with her mystery man.

No matter how hard she tried, even during their most intimate moments, she couldn't establish his identity. Of course, he was probably only contrived, but as long as he stayed around, he served as the driving impetus for losing weight. Real or not, she enjoyed their time together and the attention he paid her, but sadly, she knew one day the dreams were bound to end and she'd be alone again.

A strange feeling of dread grew in the pit of her stomach. How could she be affected so deeply by losing someone she didn't even know? Was she going crazy? The emotions that overcame her baited her back to her old ways. She started for the kitchen, but stopped short. "No way, Faith. You've made a commitment to change and you're going to stick to it."

She pictured her hunky lover's rock-hard abs and those baby blues...and the fact that he only had eyes for her. She returned to the bedroom and changed into something more comfortable. The pull-on pants she donned felt a little looser. She smiled and checked the clock to see how many hours until bedtime.

****

Faith stepped off the scales and stifled a happy giggle. She'd finally lost fifty pounds and people at work told her every day how fantastic she looked.

"Wow, that's great." The nurse congratulated her. "You've achieved so much in just over three months. It won't be long before you reach your goal."

A smile blossomed on Faith's face. "I know. My boyfriend is so pleased. You should meet him. He's so handsome...."

The lie rolled off her tongue with ease. She hadn't really been totally untruthful. Even if he existed only in her dreams, he was real to her. Thankfully the woman in white didn't press for details.

A fixed grin remained on her face as she hurried back to work. Fifty pounds? Holy cow! She finally saw the results of her hard work. She'd bought new clothes and had her hair shortened and blonde highlights added. A handsome man on the bus made her day with a wink. Although she glowed inside, she ignored his brazen flirting because she didn't want to cheat on her virile night visitor. He was the one who made giving up her favorite chocolate shakes worth the sacrifice...and his visits provided all the sugar she needed...and it wasn't even fattening.

Even the people she thought never noticed her, kept her motivated with their compliments. Funny, now that she thought about it, her dream lover hadn't intimated she'd lost weight.

At her desk, she pulled a manuscript from a growing stack and buried herself in a new romance. For a change, she likened herself to the heroine instead of wishing for her life to change.

****

Faith arrived early at work and nabbed the phone book again, searching the yellow pages, but this time for hypnotherapists. She'd researched the Internet and discovered other people with episodes similar to her dreams...all supposedly caused by repressed memories. The bond between her and her dream lover remained strong. His attentive nature and adoring looks made her believe in love...in her special connection to him. Repressed memories? She'd never met anyone like him, of that she was sure.

Nila proved to be a good listener, but never offered any input. Faith raved about the strange connection every time they got together, but her friend just stared at her, disbelief etched on her face. If she thought Faith was berserk, she didn't say anything. The only help she'd provided was when she jokingly suggested hypnotherapy. Wonder how she'd feel when she discovered Faith was taking her recommendation seriously?

Feeling a tad ridiculous, Faith dialed the digits and made an appointment. How would she react if the therapist told her she'd gone stark-raving mad?

****

A week after making the appointment, Faith sat

in Dr. Nigel Bollinger's office. Her stomach churned with apprehension. Had anyone foretold her being here, seeking a glimpse into her past, Faith would call them crazy. But here she sat, wringing her hands and shrugging to ease the tension knotted in her shoulders. The opening door startled her. She sprung to attention like a soldier meeting a commanding officer…except she remained in her chair.

"Ms. Oliver?"

Faith's breath caught in her throat. She didn't expect the doctor to summon her personally, and his eyes were as blue as a bottomless pool. Dark, wavy locks framed a smooth and tanned face. That face…the one from her dreams.

She stood on wobbly legs. "I'm Faith Oliver."

"Come with me please." The deep timbre of his voice raised goose bumps on her arms.

Following him down a carpeted hallway, her gaze locking first on his muscled shoulders then down to an equally firm ass and thighs. Her panties grew damp and her heart hitched. How could this man visit her in dreams and then act as though he'd never met her before?

At his office, Faith considered running away, but took a deep breath and entered. Even if she didn't discover the reason for her nightly visitor, she'd at least spend time with his clone.

The shades were drawn. A small lamp on a

corner table and the calm beige coating the walls created a relaxing ambiance. The mahogany finish on the doctor's desk barely showed beneath mounds of paper. A comfortable-looking chaise and his large chair were the only other furnishings, but serene paintings of seascapes and period art decorated the walls. One in particular caught her gaze—a southern couple dressed in their finest.

Faith walked closer to admire the pair—he in a pristine uniform, complete with a bright red sash, and his partner in a beautiful ivory ball gown. The woman held an open fan inches below her chin and flashed a coy smile. A small bronze plaque at the frame's bottom identified the painting as *Emancipation Ball* by Fredrick Dumas. The artwork touched a familiar nerve in Faith.

"Please, have a seat on the couch and make yourself comfortable." The doctor's voice drew her attention to him. "I'm going to ask a few questions before we get started."

Faith fidgeted beneath the blueness of his eyes. His attitude remained purely professional. Did she expect anything more?

Despite the urge to escape her discomfort and the need for him to call out her name as he did so often in dreams, Faith sat. She swiveled and stretched out on the blue suede fabric, wondering how awesome she'd feel if he came and lay beside her.

Instead, the doctor pulled his chair closer, sat,

and crossed his long legs. One ankle rested atop the opposite knee, and he propped his notepad on his limb. "So, what answers are you seeking here today?"

Her mind drew a blank, and she scrambled to find a proper response. How in the heck did one answer a single question without ending up in a straight jacket?

"I...I've been having dreams." Nervousness quivered in her voice. "Very strange dreams I don't understand."

"Tell me about them," he urged, his pen poised over the tablet resting on his leg.

She inhaled deeply and with determined slowness, released the breath. "The dreams started months ago. Every night, the same man comes to me and...." Tenseness halted her words.

"Go on. It's okay. You don't have to worry about anything you divulge within these confines. Everything is strictly confidential."

Confidential maybe, but what if he declared her mad? "All right." Her chest rose and fell with another deep breath. "In my dreams, a man comes to me and makes love like he knows me...like he expects me to recognize him, but I don't. We don't talk, but what he does to me feels completely normal. How can I continue to allow him to invade my bed when I don't even know his name?"

"Does he know yours?" Dr. tapped his pen

against his cheek.

"I honestly don't know. He's never spoken to me. Our relationship requires no words…no explanations, at least for him. Everything transpires through thought. Tell me, Doctor, am I crazy?"

He smiled, placed both feet on the floor and sat forward. "I highly doubt it. Our dreams usually have meaning." He leaned back and crossed his legs again. "Now, let's continue. Is there anything about him that stands out in your mind?"

No way was she mentioning his ample endowment; instead she turned her head and stared at the ceiling, mentally drawing her lover's image in her mind. "Several nights passed before I even noticed his face. I guess because I was so shocked by…well, I'm sure you get the picture."

"And…? Please go on."

"Y…you bear a very striking resemblance to him." She blurted the words out, regretting now the doctor really thought her ready for the loony bin."

He chuckled. "A great many people share similarities. I see nothing strange about that."

With his answer, she found relaxation against the back of the chaise. The tension flooded from her muscles and filtered through her fingertips. "Did you notice the shocked look on my face when you opened the door?"

"No more so than any other patient who visits

for the first time." He jotted a note on his pad and bade her continue with her dream.

"Faith relayed as much as she could recall until the doctor checked his wristwatch. "I hate to interrupt you, but since we only have a short time left for this appointment, I'm going to give you some homework."

She pushed a stray hair from her face, swiveled, and sat up. "Homework? A long time has passed since I heard that term."

"Nothing terribly time-consuming." His assurance came with a heart-stopping smile. "What I want you to do is keep a journal next to your bed and upon waking, write down every single thing you recall about your dreams. I'll see you next week, so you should have compiled enough information to help me assess your situation when I put you under."

"Under?"

"Hypnosis. The reason you came to me. His grin revealed a slight dimple.

"Oh, of course." Damn his blue eyes for reflecting the light, and damn him for having a dimple identical to her lover's. She'd come here hoping to find out about repressed memories, now the term, 'transference of affection" seemed a possible side effect.

****

The phone rang as Faith returned from her visit with Dr. Bollinger. She tossed her purse and journal on the sofa and answered. Nila was on the other end.

"Hey, you wanna go to a costume ball with me next Friday?"

Faith wrinkled her nose. "Not really. What kind of dance is fun without a date? I can't believe you want to go. You used to be a loner like me. What happened?"

"That's just it. I get sick of being alone, and the idea of dressing up and hiding who I am appealed to me. I suppose you'll want to stay home and go to bed."

Her last remark smacked of sarcasm and hit a nerve in Faith. "So, you don't believe I have a dream lover. Well, while you play dress up and hope someone asks you to dance, I'll be home all comfy and warm, locked in someone's arms...and we won't be dancing." She said goodbye and hung up, feeling disappointed that somewhere she and her confidante had drifted apart. Could it be the weight loss that came between them?

She sat, her guilt growing over turning down her best friend's offer. If the shoe had been on the other foot, Nila would have gone, just to be supportive. Maybe the change had nothing to do with her friend.

The more she thought, the more she decided a break from the strange dreams ruling her nights and the memories occupying her waking hours might be what she needed. Especially after meeting Dr. Bollinger, her mind waivered from a nameless lover to a handsome therapist. Two men in her life and neither were within her grasp. Weariness plagued her. The stress of the day and her plan to attempt to get her nocturnal visitor's name begged her to sleep.

Faith readied for bed, eyeing the journal on her nightstand. She crawled beneath her covers and turned off the lamp, reminding herself to pay attention to *his* features, how *he* dressed, and most of all to try and talk to *him*.

She rolled over into a more comfortable position and pulled the blanket up to her chin. Honestly, talking to herself had gotten to be a bad habit. Maybe the costume ball wasn't such a bad idea after all. She'd call Nila tomorrow and accept the invite.

****

Faith rolled her eyes at the assortment of old-fashioned lingerie littering her bed. She picked up a corset and dangled it in the air before Nila. "How in the world did women tolerate wearing this stuff? Thank goodness, all I complain about on a daily basis is pantyhose, but after seeing all this, they don't seem quite so awful." Stripping down to her own undergarments, she first put on the knee-length chemise that covered her torso. Next were pantaloons. Afterwards, she donned a camisole and struggled with the small fastening eyelets. "Geez Louise, I need smaller fingers to get hold of these things. Help me out, will you Nila?"

With her friend's help, she prepared for the corset. Holding it again, this time by two fingers, she examined it. "How the hell does this thing work?"

Nila nabbed it and wrapped the binding garment around Faith's waist and began tugging. "This is how. Take a deep breath so I can tighten the laces."

Faith took in a huge breath and held it until she was sure her face was blue. She exhaled in a gasp. "Hurry up, before I faint."

Nila finished and stepped back. "My God, your waist looks so tiny."

Shaking her head, Faith rubbed her hands along the tightness of the corset. "It should look small after you practically squeezed me to death."

"Yeah? Well how come I'm the one who's huffing and puffing? I'm going home to change while I still have the energy."

Watching her friend's ample backend barely clear the doorjamb made Faith sad. Not long had passed since she'd been in that same shape. No matter how bad she felt for Nila, she'd long ago learned through her own journey that you can't change someone else unless they participate, and clearly, Nila wasn't ready.

Faith turned her attention to the mirror. Here she stood, trussed up like a turkey and wondering why she subjected herself to the torture of something she knew was bound to be boring. Swiveling from side-to-side, she hoped the corset laces would become looser and ease their pinching.

Holding her breath, she stepped into the boned hoop, the final undergarment. With the waist tied in place to support her gown's full skirt, she dropped the dress over her head…an emerald green beauty with a low-cut bodice. She headed for the bathroom to do her hair and make-up before she stole a peek in the full-length mirror.

With hands on hips, she stood before the looking glass. The gown featured her best assets, and her shrunken waist enlarged the appearance of her breasts. Velvet ribbons of lighter green rimmed each cap sleeve and formed a delicate bow. She'd pulled her grown-out tresses back behind her ears and donned a matching, crocheted snood. Who would have thought something as quaint as a hairnet could look so fetching. The fringe of bangs across her forehead and wisps framing her face added just the touch of femininity needed for the head covering. The contrasting colors of her outfit perfectly complimented her complexion and hair. Faith lifted her skirt and did a pirouette. She'd been lucky to find something so marvelous on short notice.

She approached her bureau for the final touches. With perfect jewels adorning her earlobes and a thin strand of emerald ribbon circling her neck, she looked the part of a genuine southern belle. Wearing a bright color provided a welcome change. For so long she'd worn nothing but black because she believed it slimming, but she'd retired her lint magnet wardrobe about sixty pounds ago. Although she still wore a size fourteen, and some considered anything over a ten, large, the mirror showed an entirely different opinion. She spun again, her skirt rustling against her hoop, and the breeze stirring the bows on her shoulders. Reminded of the painting she'd recently viewed, Faith fantasized over living in the Civil War era.

From nowhere, the name "Joshua" flashed through her mind again.

A frown creased her forehead. Who the heck was he, and why did she keep conjuring up his name? Had she read about him in a manuscript? When no acknowledging bells sounded, she hurried to the nightstand and made an entry in her journal. Maybe Dr. Bollinger could help.

She glanced at the clock near her journal. Almost time to meet Nila. Faith rushed to the bathroom and dabbed some perfume behind her ears and on the tiny pulsing spot in the hollow of her neck.

Her smile faded when she realized she'd agreed to go to a single's dance. When had she gotten so desperate?

She mentally reminded herself she'd agreed for Nila's sake, and this outing might provide the perfect opportunity to meet a 'real' man. She'd view the occasion as her debut into society. Snickering, she reached for the aerosol can on the back of the toilet, sprayed her hair one last time, and then added a little more blush. Excitement finally set in.

****

Faith followed Nila into a festive ballroom where only a handful of costume-clad people mingled. Pausing near the entrance, Faith admired the balloon bouquets and bright crepe paper decorations. Standing, she found comfort. The ride to the dance had been an adventure, to say the least.

Nila motioned her over to an empty table and Faith joined her. She tugged at her side where the corset bit into her and gathered her full skirt in preparation to sit. "Now I know why women who wore these hoops rode in wagons." Faith struggled to get the hoop under the table without it sweeping upward. "I can hardly wait to cram myself back in your car. It's a wonder you could see to drive."

Nila rolled her eyes. "All you've done is

complain. First you didn't want to come; now you're nagging me about how you got here. Get over it. I snagged us a table right next to the dance floor and guys are bound to notice you. What more can I do? "

Faith hung her head. "You're right. Must be close to my time of the month. I've been a hag, haven't I?" She adjusted her skirt and inched her chair forward. "Well, I'm here and I might as well make the best of the evening. I've lost all the weight, spent money I couldn't afford on this outfit, and now I'm anxious to see if my investment was worth having no food the rest of the month." She chuckled. "Oh, by the way, Nila, you make a great looking butler. I hardly recognized you."

"Thanks, but if I'd given a little more thought to my costume, I could have come as Rhett Butler."

"Frankly, dahling, I don't give a damn." Faith couldn't resist using an exaggerated southern drawl, then dug in her rented reticule for one more era piece. She unfurled a colorful fan and flicking her wrist, moved the pleated paper back and forth while peering over it at her friend. "Really, you look just like a man. I only hope no one thinks you're my date."

The DJ announced the first song of the evening. Faith sat straighter in her chair, crossed her ankles and tried to relax...no easy feat in a pinching corset. Despite her best attempts to compose, her palms grew wet inside her gloves. She tugged at the fingertips until the elbow-high encasements came off, and then she discreetly ran her hands along her skirt. All the while, she kept an eye on the growing number of costumed men around the room and wondered which one might approach and ask her to dance.

Song after song played and still no one came forward. Why had she spent so much time and effort on losing weight when she was still invisible to those of the opposite sex? Several women had stopped by the table and admired her costume, but when the band announced another "take ten," she tired of being there and wanted to leave.

She'd run out of small talk during the last break and sat quietly, toying with her empty glass. Nila's peeved glance at the incessant clinking clued Faith of the annoyance.

"Sorry." Faith folded her hands in her lap and released a deep breath.

Her friend turned and furrowed her brow. "I suppose you're ready to go?"

"In all honesty, I've had all the fun I can stand for one evening."

"Didn't you enjoy yourself at all? Wasn't being here better than staying home watching TV again? I liked the music, didn't you?"

Faith stood and picked up her reticule. "Yeah, the music was dee-vine, but my feet are killing me from all that dancing I did."

"You don't have to be sarcastic. If you want to go, we'll go."

"Sorry, Nila. I know it isn't your fault. At least at home, I can go to sleep and dream about someone who cares about me...at least I think it's me. I'm sorry I wasn't a better companion."

****

Faith tugged the hooped petticoat from beneath her gown. "It doesn't matter if you lost weight," she ranted. "You're still too fat and no one wants to dance with you. No One!" She wrestled out of her dress, and struggled to unlace her corset. Nila had done a great job of fastening the ties, but once removed, Faith was left in her pantaloons and chemise. She tossed the discarded clothing down to the foot and plopped in the middle of the bed and pondered the disappointing evening.

Losing weight was supposed to make a difference, not disappoint her, but she'd been so rude to Nila and probably pretty childish. She'd call her friend tomorrow and apologize...and maybe take her out for dinner. Nila always enjoyed good food.

Faith headed for the kitchen, opened the refrigerator, and scanned the bare shelves. Pickings were slim since she'd been sticking to her diet, but her disappointment in the evening called out for something good, rich and fattening…but what?

A chocolate shake.

She grabbed the remaining milk and opened the cupboard next to her for the cocoa. There wasn't ice cream to be found, but she could add a banana and whatever else that appealed to her. While in a mixing frenzy, she caught a glance of her reflection in the oven door. She huffed out her disdain over giving into cravings, put the chocolate away, and set the milk back in the fridge. She munched on the banana and shuffled back to her room. She wasn't ready to give up on herself just yet.

Tears streamed down her cheeks. She'd expected so much more from the evening. Silent crying turned to sobs, and she collapsed onto the bed, curling herself into a ball. She clutched the pillowcase as months of pent-up frustration and sacrifice found released. When all her tears were shed, she'd vowed to find a way to be complete without a man—even a make-believe one.

Sliding off the bed, she changed into her nightgown and crawled beneath the covers. Hopefully tonight there'd be no dreams. What she once enjoyed now gave her reasons to doubt herself.

****

Faith had taken the day off for her

appointment. She sat in the waiting room, clutching her journal, and puzzled why her dream man hadn't visited once since the costume ball. Had he sensed her unwillingness to welcome him?

An old saying rang in her mind. "Be careful what you wish for." Was this what she really wanted? At least in her boring life, *he* had created excitement and eased her loneliness. His absence left her without the loving attentiveness she craved.

"Ms. Oliver, nice to see you again." Dr. Bollinger appeared in the doorway. "C'mon back, please."

Faith followed him into his office and took her place on the chaise lounge. The doctor's appealing attributes kept her from focusing on the reason she'd come. She offered up her journal. "I've put down everything I thought might be helpful. Unfortunately, I haven't had any dreams in days, so a lot of entries are from memory. I'm a little embarrassed to bare my soul to you."

"No need. We all have sexual thoughts and needs." He studied her notes for a moment, and then glanced up at her. "Ms. Oliver—"

"Could you please call me Faith? I'd feel a little less like my mother."

"Okay, Faith…I want you to stretch out, close your eyes and listen to my voice."

She raised her feet from the floor and reclined.

"As I begin to count backwards from ten, you're

going to feel so relaxed you won't be able to open your eyes. Ten…your limbs are growing heavy, so heavy they want to sink into the fabric beneath you…nine…like a candle in the sunlight, you're melting into a pool of relaxation…eight…you hear everything I say, and you will remember…seven…nothing I say or anything you see will frighten you. You're safe and nothing can hurt you…six…you're so sleepy, sleep…five… sleep…four…deeper in sleep…three, two, one… deep, deep asleep."

Faith crinkled her brow in an attempt to open her eyes but failed. Her lids were leaden, and every other part of her body felt like an unraveled garden hose. She'd never felt so relaxed—and against her will, at that.

Dr. Bollinger's voice, deep and soothing, proved she could be hypnotized despite her disbelief. Her breathing came soft and easy.

"Okay, Faith, now, we're going to travel backwards." His melodic voice invaded her serenity.

"You're no longer in 2004. I want you to visualize the years as we pass through them—2003, 2002, 2001…tell me, what's happening."

Tears dampened her cheeks, but she couldn't lift a hand to brush them away. "She's dead….my mother's gone. Now I have no one." Panic added a quiver to Faith's shaken voice. "What am I going to do?"

"You'll be fine, Faith. It's okay to mourn her loss. She was wonderful to you and you loved her very much. How are you dealing with her death? What brings you comfort? You can move your arms now, if you need to."

"I'm eating because I don't have anything but food to make me feel better. My mother always makes such great meals." Faith reached out her arms. "Don't leave me, mom. Come back to me."

"Faith, the pain is fading, fading, gone. Now, we're going back further...back, back, back to 1986. You're around ten now. Tell me what you see."

The feel of a smile blossomed on her lips, and she gave a happy sigh. "Momma, I see momma."

"What's she doing, Faith?"

She gave a childish giggle and clapped her hands. "She's cooking my favorite dinner. I got my report card today, and she's so proud of me."

"I'm proud of you, too. Do you like getting rewards?"

"Oh...yes, I love when Momma cooks something special for me. Sometimes, when she can afford it, she buys me candy, or takes me to the movies. I'd rather have her good food. Momma works, you know, and I stay by myself now that I'm a big girl. I can't let anyone in, Momma says, but when she gets home and we're together, we'll share a good dinner...and we laugh."

"You must be a very good girl, Faith. I'm sure your mother loves you. Now, I want you to follow my voice and move on with me. Can you do that?"

Little girl snuffles shook her body. "No, I want to stay with Momma."

"Things will be fine, I promise. You'll always have your mother in your heart, but we must move one. No more tears, don't be scared and continue to listen to my voice."

His calmness soothed Faith. Her tears subsided.

"I'm reaching for your hand, Faith. Take mine and let's go back...back, back beyond the time you remember...back beyond your birth, conception, to a life you had before you were Faith Oliver. Return to a time where you're no longer held by memories of life as you know it this moment. Release those old memories, Faith, and search your mind for new ones."

In the shrouding darkness, Faith strained to see. In the distance, a speck of white beckoned and she approached. Nearer, the light brightened and her mouth gaped in awe of the scenery. In her hypnotic state, she turned full-circle and surveyed the surrounding splendor. Seeing such beauty, she held her breath.

She stood before a large colonial mansion—a place she'd only seen in pictures. Tall columns created a marvelous entrance to the majestic front doors and lent support to an outside balcony. She craned her neck to see the intricate carvings on the snowy-colored pillars that dwarfed her. The honeysuckle growing on the porch railing permeated the air with a sweet smell. "Ohhh," was all she could utter.

"What, Faith? Share with me what you see."

"A beautiful house...so big, so white, with columns in front. There are wicker chairs on the front porch and a full balcony overhead."

"What else, Faith? Look around."

"Land, lots of land...green and rich. Oh, my goodness. There's a huge Weeping Willow in the front yard. I love those elegant trees.

"Is there more?"

"It's all so beautiful." She sighed. "Beyond the house, I see a barn, and lots of horses in the corral next to it."

"Do you see people?" Dr. Bollinger continued his probing.

"No, there's no one here but me. Oh, wait! Out in the field, I do see people...they appear to be working, but I can't be sure because they're so far away." She squinted. "I think they're all black."

"Do you mean black people or are they surrounded by black?"

"Black people...Negroes."

"Anyone else?"

"Wait, the front door is opening. Someone is coming out onto the porch. Oh, she's so pretty and..."

"Tell me about her, Faith. What's she wearing?"

The woman struck a familiar chord. "She has on a long red gingham dress with a very full skirt. Her hair is golden and piled atop her head with a few loose ringlets." Faith paused and crinkled her brow.

"Does your head hurt?"

"No, the sun is very bright."

"Oh, of course it is. What's happening now?"

"The woman is shading her eyes with her hand…searching for someone perhaps."

Faith gasped. "She's looking at me."

"Don't worry. She won't hurt you."

"Maddy? She's motioning to me and is calling me Maddy."

"Okay, Faith, you've traveled far enough today." Dr. Bollinger's voice sliced the momentary silence. "Let's bring you back to present. Follow my voice and come back with me. As I count to ten, the years will whiz past until you're here and awake again. "Ten…"

The light began to fade.

"Nine, eight, seven…you have nothing to fear as you come back, all the way back."

The mansion vanished and the world blurred. An unexplainable sadness gripped at her.

"Six…you'll remember everything you've seen…five, four, three two, one…awake!"

Faith's eyes opened and adjusted to the muted

light. Too stunned by what she'd experienced, she remained silent and waited for the Doctor to offer an explanation.

He flashed her a smile. "I know you're a bit confused, but we don't have time to cover everything you've been through today. We'll meet again next week and see if we can go back and pick up where we left off."

"But...."

"I know, you want to talk about the experience now, but I have another patient waiting. If your dreams resume, log them and anything else you might want to discuss."

Frustration welled in her chest, but her time was up and there was no arguing with the clock. "I understand. Maybe it's just as well that I go now. I'm very tired and I probably wouldn't grasp anything you told me."

Dr. Bollinger stood and opened the door. "You've had quite an adventure today. Go home, get some rest, and I'll see you soon."

A zillion questions danced in her head, and she had to wait an entire week for answers. Who was Maddy and why did the woman from the mansion call her that? And what about the mysterious Joshua whose name kept creeping into her head; was he somehow associated with the past? Faith shook her head. She just wanted to go home and pretend everything was normal. If she felt puzzled before, she was really confused now.

****

Faith thrashed about in her bed. "Oh, don't stop," she begged, breathlessly. In her dream, she was pinned against the wall by her lover, and his mouth traveled the length of her arched neck, leaving butterfly kisses in the wake. He whispered words of love only she could hear.

Half awake, Faith tossed and turned, fighting the belief it wasn't his hands roaming from her thighs to her hips, and then past her waist to cup her ample breasts…to push them together and bury his face in the cleavage.

Her fingers ached to splay through his hair and offer him a swollen nipple, but she feared she wouldn't feel his suckling; that the dream would end…after all, hadn't she prayed he wouldn't return?

She hadn't meant it. His imaginary caresses ignited her deepest passion, and she wanted more. Fearful of opening her eyes lest he disappear, she balled her fists and endured the stinging pain of her nails digging into her palms. The noticeable comfort of her bed turned to stone like the wall against which she stood in the dream.

In the throes of passion, her lids fluttered open

to behold her lover. Her vision rested first on the ivory gown she wore, and then drifted to his attire. How strange? In all other dreams they had already shed their clothing. She wrestled with reality. Had he not just touched her bare body?

The trailing lips on her throat stirred feelings she couldn't fight. Relenting, she ran her hands along the back of his jacket, caressing rigid muscles through the satiny fabric. He felt so real.

"What's your name?" She whispered. "Tell me your name." Now she demanded.

He stood away from her for a moment and peered adoringly into her eyes. Clad in a uniform, beneath his jacket, an unbuttoned dress shirt hung open to the red sash around his waist. She ached to touch the matting of dark hair on his tanned chest, but took a calming breath.

"Please, please tell me your name." She prayed for an answer.

The alarm slicked through her dream and drove her lover back into the shadows. "Please….your name?" She awoke muttering her plea, and in a haze, slapped the alarm to stop the piercing noise.

She rubbed her forehead and bemoaned her fate. If only she'd had a few more minutes, she was sure he was about to reveal his identity.

Realizing it was a work day, Faith rose and went into the bathroom. While she sat on the toilet, she buried her face in her hands, trying to recapture elements of the dream she might have missed. Why had she been wearing an ivory gown one moment and not the next, and what about his uniform? What year was it?

The only thing clear in her mind was she'd seen their attire before. Her mind flashed to the portrait in Dr. Bollinger's office…especially the red sash. Was her dream love from another time and place?

She flushed the toilet and turned on the shower. As soon as she got to work, she'd surf the Internet for information on Civil War uniforms.

****

The search engine brought up more information than one could possibly scan in a lifetime. Where did she begin? Clicking on the first link, she viewed an array of modern-day army, navy, marine and air force attire. Not quite what she had in mind, although a man in uniform always turned a woman's eyes.

She entered "Civil War uniforms," to be more explicit and perused the dark blue of the northern states, from infantry to cavalry to officer. Her finger on the down arrow, she moved to confederate uniforms. The color was right, but the style wasn't. Scrolling further, her gaze rested on the exact jacket she'd seen in the painting...in her dreams—an officer's jacket. The chart alongside the screen displayed the meaning of the different colored sashes—red for lieutenant.

Thoughts spun through her mind like a spider weaving all the loose ends of its web together. She lifted her gaze from the screen and stared at the wall. Could he be the reason she was drawn to the costume shop and her disguise for the ball? Did she know him in another life?

She flashed back to the Civil War portrait, with too many coincidences and too few explanations. Her boss poked his head into the room; she jumped at the intrusion into her thoughts. "Are you finished editing Michelle Collins' manuscript?" He eyed the lack of papers in front of her and frowned.

Faith shuffled through the papers on her desk. "I...I'm almost finished." Embarrassed at having been caught at something non-work-related, her hands shook. "I'll have it done today."

"That would be nice." Her supervisor nodded and walked away, leaving Faith stunned at having lied. She hadn't even started edits, and if she wanted to meet her self-imposed deadline, she'd needed to get moving. All her personal issues had to wait, no matter how important they seemed. She searched through the manuscript pile, looking for the author's name, and pulled out the one she needed. Her gaze fixed on the title. "*Only in Dreams*. How apropos!

****

Faith took wide strides to reach Dr. Bollinger's office, eager to share her latest revelation. Her journal held as much information as possible, but far too many questions kept her writing everything down. She had a hard time distinguishing between what was real and what wasn't.

As soon as he called her name, she practically beat him to his office in her quest to stretch out on the comfort of the couch and travel back in time. Excitement set her heart to pounding and echoed in her ears. She leaned back and closed her eyes.

"So, Faith, how did things go for you this week?" His voice drew her from her ready status and she opened her eyes. He wanted to make small talk? Her jaw tense, she thrust her journal at him. "I thought you'd want to pursue the hypnosis."

"We will, we will. Just be patient." She swiveled her feet to the floor and moved her chin back and forth to ease the tension. "Very well, then. My dream lover came back, and this time and I noticed something new."

"What's that?"

"Well," she paused, her cheeks heating. "There's no other way to say this except...this time he had clothes on, and so did I...at least part of the time. I had on a ball gown and he, a uniform identical to the one in your painting." She pointed to where it hung. "I did some research—"

"Take a breath, Faith. Slow down and relax a moment."

She inhaled and released the air slowly, but if she didn't hurry, her appointment time would run out before she had a chance to tell him everything, let alone seek more answers from being hypnotized. "I'm sorry I'm so excited."

"Now that you've calmed down a bit, continue with your dream."

"So, when I got to work the next morning, I searched the web for uniforms and found the exact one he wore. Obviously, my night visitor dresses in the garb of a Confederate lieutenant."

"I notice you're still referring to the man in your dreams as 'he.' Didn't you find out a name this time?"

"No. The blasted alarm went off just as I asked him."

"Then, let's see if we can find out something today that might answer some of these questions. Get comfortable and let's begin."

Faith reclined again, resting her head against the back of the chaise. After taking another deep breath, she waited. Her heart rate notched up a few beats.

"Listen to my voice," the doctor began. "Your body is relaxing into a pool of liquid. From the count of ten...feel the heaviness of your arms and legs, and let your mind drift back...back in time. Nine, eight seven...the scenery around you is blurred as you move back...far back to where we left off. When I get to one, you will be standing in the yard...six...you see the Weeping Willow...five, four, three, two, one."

Everything was as she remembered...the majesty of the house, the lush grounds, the honeysuckle hanging heavy in the air. Had she even moved a step?

"Maddy, there you are." The blonde woman on the porch addressed Faith. "Where have you been? You'd best get inside and get yourself ready for the ball. Joshua will soon be here to escort you."

"Tell me what's happening, Faith. I see a look of confusion on your face." Dr. Bollinger's voice intruded on the moment.

"She's calling me Maddy. I have to go get dressed now."

"Go with her, and have no fear. From this moment on, you will be Maddy until I summon you back."

"Coming, Mother." Faith answered as Maddy. "I'll be right in as soon as I find just the right colored rose to match my dress."

"Oh, daughter, you've always been given to dawdling. Don't take too long."

****

"Another adventure, I'd say." Dr. Bollinger commented on Faith's excitement when he summoned her back to reality. He checked his watch. "We still have a few minutes before my next patient. Tell me about your experience."

Faith gathered her thoughts. She had to look stunned. How could she not? "I felt so at home. The house was where Maddy lived...and her mother...my mother was so beautiful. My family owned that beautiful home?

He smiled.

"The inside was every bit as beautiful as the exterior. Polished floors that glistened, mahogany banisters...elegant furniture and luxurious rugs. Oh, my family must have been very wealthy." Faith closed her eyes and blew an exhalation through pursed lips.

"Who is Joshua? You muttered his name several times."

Faith's eyes widened. "Oh my gosh. That's the name from my dreams I kept telling you about. He's Maddy's...my fiancé. We're to be married as soon as the war is over."

"And what war is that, Faith?"

"The war between the states, of course." She paused and cocked her head. "How could I possibly know so much about Maddy and her family, Dr.

Bollinger?"

He leaned forward in his chair. "Do you believe in past lives?"

Did she? Skepticism shrouded her. "I've heard talk of them, but…."

Her therapist rubbed his hands together and smiled. "Well, Faith, my dear, I believe we've tapped into a connection to your dream."

****

Faith, curled at sofa's end, her elbow resting on the cushiony arm, pondered her visit with Dr. Bollinger. Big deal, she'd discovered a past life, but that only meant Joshua never loved her; he loved Maddy—thin, fragile, and attractive Maddy, not fat, ugly Faith. Okay, so she wasn't as fat as she used to be, but she'd never look as beautiful as Maddy, that was for sure.

If Joshua came to her in a dream again, she vowed to stop the masquerade once and for all. What was the point of continuing? His nighttime visits tied to another woman, not her, and of late, her dreams only served to remind her how lonely her days had become. She rose and went to the bedroom, changed into her gown and summoned the courage to do what needed to be done.

She tossed and turned for a long time before sleep finally claimed her. Her subconscious mind called out to Joshua, and as if the last dream never ended, he appeared and held her captive with his kisses. Her resolve diminished, and she surrendered to his advances. His hands sought her and found her bare breasts, and his hardness pressed against her groin.

The quickening of her heart fluttered against the confining bodice of her gown. How could Joshua massage her bare skin? Her mind screamed at her to realize she dreamed something that wasn't real. Conscious thoughts summoned her to awaken.

"I love you, Maddy. " A deep sensual voice summoned her back into his arms. "I want to make love to you forever."

He'd spoken for the first time. Until now, their exchanges had been only lustful moans and groans. Dare she speak back?

In the throes of sleep and wakefulness, she attempted what she vowed. "Why do you call me Maddy? That isn't my name."

Joshua chuckled. "What else should I call you? Do you prefer your given name, Madeline?"

"But...my name is...."

His tongue lapped at the hollow of her throat, sending shock waves down her spine.

"My name is Faith."

"Then I shall call you whatever you like, but now, my darling, kiss me and mean it. Tomorrow I leave to take my place near the front and see this battle to the end. Tonight, my love, I'm Lieutenant Joshua Hartley, at your service."

"But, you don't understand." Faith writhed away from his grasp. "I'm not who you think I am. None of this makes sense. How can you love me when you don't even know me? I look nothing like the woman whose name you call me. I'm fat in comparison…and ugly." She waited for his response, her breath halted.

"Not to me, my darling, not to me. When I look at you, I see the woman I love." He drew her back into his embrace.

Passion wiped away her senses. While his lips covered her mouth in a deep and probing kiss, she snaked her leg around his body and drew him closer. Her fingers grasped the taut flesh of his shoulders…until her conscious mind again screamed for her to awaken.

More awake than asleep, she pushed Joshua away, holding him at arm's length. "Don't, please. You can't keep invading my every sleeping hour and keep making me love you…pretend you love me.

His brows rose, and he held her forearms firmly. "But, I do love you, Maddy."

"I'm not Maddy! Look at me! I mean *really* look at me. I'm tired of being someone else in my dreams. Can't you understand what you're doing to me? I'm Faith, not the thin, sexy woman you desire and see when I sleep."

He released her and hung his head. "I don't understand."

"I can't continue this charade. When I sleep, I become Maddy, the person you really love. She isn't me. Please, Joshua, don't do this anymore. I can't stand knowing you're just a dream in love with someone else."

"But I love you, and I'm not a dream. I'm real, and we belong together." He tried pulling her close again.

"No." She pulled away. "You aren't real. Please leave me alone."

Her sobbing and thrashing about brought her wide-awake. She sat upright and covered her face. "Oh, Lord, what have I done?"

The taste of his kiss still lingered on her lips; her skin still tingled from his touch. Was this what lunacy was like?

Faith swallowed hard, looked around the empty room and wiped away her tears. She had to let him go. He was nothing more than a figment of an imagination from the past.

Sadness formed a lump in her throat and she choked it down. She reached for her journal, certain she was going to make the last entry about him—her wonderfully handsome, Joshua.

****

The week prior to her appointment passed with the slowness of a snail's movement before Faith was back in the doctor's reception area. She drummed her fingers on her journal while she waited.

The interior door opened. "Hi, Faith. Nice to see you again." She stifled a groan, seeing the notable resemblance he shared with Joshua.

"Nice to see you again, Dr. Bollinger. Yes, seeing him was what she wanted, but if he only resembled anyone but Joshua…. She followed him to his office and took her usual position on the sofa.

"So, tell me, have you had more dreams?"

Faith swallowed the growing lump in her throat. "I have, and I'm more confused than ever. Last week, I became Maddy during our session, and that is the name Joshua called me in our last encounter. Obviously, he's the very same Joshua that Maddy's mother talked about." She fixed him with a hopeful stare. "What does this all mean, Doctor Bollinger? Am I Maddy or is he fixated on me because he thinks I am?"

The doctor shook his head. "I'm not quite sure, but I think we can find out. Relax and let's go back in time…only this session, we're going to move a little forward and start where we left off. Are you ready?"

Relax? Ready? The very words increased her hesitation. Air filled her lungs and became trapped by nerves. What if she didn't like what she discovered? Still, she had to know or all the time and money spent on these sessions would be a waste. She released her pent-up breath. "Yes. I'm ready."

"Good, then feel your eyes growing heavy, your arms and legs turning to lead, but your breathing is slow and steady. Ten, nine eight…we're traveling back to the mansion. You're standing beneath a beautiful Weeping Willow. The cool air caressing your cheek…seven, six, five, four, three, two…you're home and your name is Maddy. One.

In her mind, she pivoted, her arms sweeping the breeze. "The cool air is refreshing, and I hear crickets chirping in the bushes. The sunset is so beautiful…a painter's pallet."

"Maddy, can you hear me?" Dr. Bollinger's voice drifted back in time.

"Yes, I hear you."

"Then, follow my voice…we're going to move forward one week…relax and allow your mind to drift. You've been to the Officer's Ball and you're in your room. What are you doing?"

"I'm crying." She swiped at tears. "Joshua has gone to war and I miss him so. I worry he won't come back to me, but he promised no matter what happens, we'll find one another."

"Let's go forward one month, two months, three months…are you with me, Maddy? Tell me where you are."

"Oh, my God." Faith's hand massaged the pain in Maddy's breaking heart. "Our plantation is in ruin. The Union soldiers have set torches to it, and everything we owned is destroyed and the home is nothing but a burned out shell. The beautiful countryside is nothing but smoldering ashes now."

She rubbed her stomach. "I'm so hungry. We all are. There's nothing to eat. The marauders set fire to the fields cleaned out the garden and took all the food Mother canned. Father tried to fight them...he and the few slaves who hadn't run off...and the soldiers beat them badly. Mother is tending to Papa's wounds and praying he lives." Tears expressed her worry and anguish.

"Listen to me, Maddy," the doctor interrupted the disastrous scene. "Move forward....six months...one year. Drift with me and look into your future and Faith's past. Where are you?"

"I'm in Atlanta, living with Aunt Mary. Mother and I came here after Papa passed. I lost my beloved Joshua, too...his whole regiment wiped out...." The pain of her losses etched her voice. "Now, I'm destined to be an old maid because I shall never love another like I loved my dashing Lieutenant. The last post I received from him assured me of eternal love, but I guess 'twas not to be."

"It's time to come back now. Follow my voice

and begin the journey home. Ten, you'll leave all the hurt and pain behind...nine, you'll remember everything about Maddy and hold her memory in your mind...eight, you're coming back in time, back to the present...seven, six, five, four...almost here...three...two...one. Open your eyes, Faith."

She rubbed her eyes with balled fists, and then focused on the doctor. "I've never been so happy to see someone in my whole life."

"Why's that?"

"The Civil War era was horrid. Maddy might be thin and beautiful, but I've got so much more than she ever dreamt of having. I never thought I'd say this, but I'm happy to be me."

The Doctor chuckled. "Good to hear, but—"

"There's that 'but' again, telling me my time is up."

"You're right, but, if you can, I'd like you to come back tomorrow so we can sum everything up. I want to clarify your experiences for you and explain why I believe you're having recurrent dreams."

****

So as not to interfere with her work schedule, Faith held Dr. Bollinger's last appointment of the day. All during the day, she'd thought about nothing but Joshua, and when she followed the doctor to his office, rather than stretching out on his familiar couch, she sat in a chair across the desk from him. Her palms turned damp.

"You look nervous, Faith." Doctor Bollinger flipped through his notebook.

"I'm anxious to hear what you have to say, but afraid to listen. Does that make sense?"

"After what you've been through, I do understand, but what happened is a normal progression. Most people don't take time to explore the impetus behind their dreams or nightmares, nor do they believe in kindred spirits. Do you?"

"I suppose after this, I do, but I'm not entirely sure I understand them."

The therapist cupped his chin. "Let's see if I can clarify by using your dream as an example."

Faith leaned forward.

"Many, including me, believe Life is a cycle that can and often is repeated. When you pass from one life, you begin anew." As he spoke, he tapped his pencil against his desk, but when Faith's gaze moved to the source of the noise, he ceased.

"Sorry, nervous habit." He laughed.

"Do go on, please."

"From your experiences, I surmise that during the Civil War era you lived as a young woman named Maddy who was engaged to a young man in the Confederate army. Since we didn't extensively explore your life as Maddy, I have no idea when and how you passed, but we do know Joshua died in the war. I assume from your heartfelt emotions during the regression, you truly suffered the loss of your loved ones. This leads me to your compulsion for overeating. I truly understand how you would gravitate to eating after surviving a war when food was scarce, plus to lessen the pain of the memories you maintain from Maddy's energy within you. Her soul is your soul, and you ease the pain you feel with food. Those from one's past can be an energetic force and often adhere to people familiar and comfortable. You and Madeline are kindred spirits, bonded for eternity."

The story the doctor told was as good as any manuscript Faith had ever read. She inched to the edge of her chair. "But what about the dreams?"

"The notes in your journal and the events during your sessions reveal that Joshua's declaration of never-ending love is the cause. His spirit traveled through the ages to find you again."

Faith shook her head. "NO, he traveled back to find Maddy, but instead, found me. For what purpose?"

"I honestly don't think we'll ever know unless Joshua reveals his reasons to you. You are Maddy in spirit, and the woman he loves, but Faith shares that spirit."

"But why does he make love to me like I'm

Maddy. Our bodies are nothing alike."

"I know you wanted a more precise reason for your recurrent dreams, but the proverbial ball is in Joshua's court. I don't know if the dreams will continue or not, but I hope you've gained some understanding of what brought him to you in the first place."

Faith leaned back and sighed. "I do understand up to a point, but I'm still confused. I'm pained to think Joshua believes I'm his true love, Maddy, and even more, that I've fallen in love with someone who isn't real."

Dr. Bollinger walked around the desk, extended a hand, and helped Faith to her feet. "Oh, he's real, just not in the physical sense." He preceded her to the door and opened it. "I'm sorry I couldn't provide your perfect ending, Faith. I'm afraid we went as far as we could to explain your dreams."

"You've been most helpful, Doctor. I guess what happens from here on depends on me and Joshua."

****

Faith stilled her alarm and shuffled into the bathroom. A whole week had passed since her last doctor's appointment and she'd not had one dream. Joshua had gone from her life. She'd never again enjoy being held in his arms, tasting his kisses. How was she going to get through life without him? She'd never felt this close to heartbreak since her mother died.

Red-ringed eyes peered back from the mirror over the sink as Faith brushed her teeth. Tousled hair framed her face, but did nothing to hide her swollen eyelids or mask the dark circles accentuating her pale skin.

"Be careful what you wish for." Her mumbling reminded her how she'd complained about the dreams and how unsettling they'd been. Joshua had been visiting a spirit and unless there was some way to make him real, life without him was over. Tears again misted her eyes.

****

Two weeks and no dreams…of any kind. Her workdays kept her submersed in romance manuscripts and did nothing to ease the pain of missing Joshua.

"Good morning, Faith." The voice of someone passing her doorway drew her attention. Management had filled a vacancy with a man every woman in the office considered eye candy, but she wasn't going to play the fool again by believing his smiles meant anything. Joshua had never loved Faith…just the thinner, more attractive spirit within her. Besides, there was no way someone that looked like Todd Miller would flirt with her.

"Good morning." She went right back to proofing a manuscript, despite being reminded of her pain. By five o'clock, she was more than ready to leave and shocked to find Todd waiting for her in the hallway.

"Mind if I walk you out?"

She made a sweeping glance behind her to assure his words weren't directed at someone else. "M…me? Fine."

He stood and made small talk with her until her bus came, and even mentioned they should share lunch some time. The entire time they chatted, Faith saw Joshua's face and heard his voice.

"This is my ride," she announced. "Thanks for…well, just thanks."

He chuckled. "See you tomorrow." He pulled his overcoat higher on his neck as he walked away, and the chilling Boston breeze picked up.

Faith stepped onto the bus, pondering why Todd had waited for her. Her thoughts quickly turned to Joshua and she relived some of their passionate moments. Maybe, just maybe he hadn't really deserted her.

The bus ground to a halt at her stop, and Faith exited. The weather held a distinct chill, and the days had grown shorter. With the sun far below the buildings, her thin sweater did little to warm her. She made a beeline for the complex door and darted inside.

The carpeted hallway masked her footsteps. She passed Nila's apartment, and resisted the urge to knock. Although they usually compared their days, Faith had not mentioned Joshua or her lack of dreams, and tonight she was just too tired to stop by. She'd slept little during the past few weeks. Tonight would undoubtedly be different.

In her apartment, she popped a low-calorie TV dinner into the oven while she changed into her nightgown. When the oven beeped, she put her meal on a tray and sat on the couch. Although she flipped channels, she found nothing to keep her awake. Although a glance at the clock showed only seven p.m., exhaustion summoned her to bed.

****

Faith's head barely touched the pillow and she was out...or was she in Dr. Bollinger's office? She tossed and turned, the dark of sleep she craved turning to light, and either she or Maddy, stood on the front porch of an estate in Georgia. Across the lawn, beneath the umbrella of a tree, stood her love in his uniform. His horse, tethered to a tree branch, grazed in contentment. Joshua beckoned her to join him.

His hat rested on the saddle horn, a soft breeze fluttered through his dark hair, leaving a stray strand draping down his forehead. Her fingers ached to brush his locks back into place…to enjoy his embrace. So handsome in his Lieutenant's garb, he supported his saber at his waist with his flowing red sash.

Her feet skimmed the ground in her quest to reach him. Where had he been, why he was alive, was it Maddy he loved…or Faith?

In his arms again, her heart pounded like a drummer leading a charge. She inhaled the masculine scent of him, reveled in his touch. Her lips parted to receive his probing tongue while his embrace tightened. The flame that had grown cold from his absence reignited.

He stepped back from, holding her at arm's length. "I've missed you, my darling."

She started to speak but he held a finger to her lips.

"Hush, my love. I know you have questions, but my time here is brief. Let me drink in your beauty to sustain me until we're together again."

"But…."

He placed a note in her hand and closed here fingertips around it. "No words, just read what I've penned and remember, I shall always love you."

Joshua lifted the hand holding his message and sealed his missive with a kiss.

After plucking the reins from the branch, he placed his hat firmly on his head and mounted his sturdy roan. "I love you with all that I am," he said, while gazing down at her. "Don't ever doubt that."

He galloped away, leaving her with unanswered questions and a breaking heart. Her hand tightened on his note. She unrolled the piece of paper and read:

My dearest Faith,

I finally realize Maddy's memory is but a portion of what I love about you. My life and time with her have passed, but by finding you, I pray to move forward and enjoy love again. Although the special moments we shared were only in dreams, I had no other way with which to connect to you.

I'm here, in your time in space. Just as Madeline's spirit lives on, I, too, have found my place in your world. You have only to find me.

I will wait for you, my love. Come quickly as I'm missing you already.

Yours forever,

Joshua

"Please, don't leave me. Don't go!" Her own screams woke her. She bolted upright and scanned the room.

Her heartbeat pulsed in her head. Was it true? Was Joshua real or did she only dream he was because she wanted him to be?

She turned on the lamp to assure she was alone

and in her own room. The clock showed only an hour before her alarm sounded. The dream she'd just experienced coupled with the answers from Dr. Bollinger confused her even more. Oh, she understood about kindred spirits, but how much of this vision was based on desire to keep Joshua in her life? But how could she? He'd died in the war. Had he been saying goodbye and going to his death? Tears spilled down her cheeks.

How could she make sense of this? A lump formed in her throat and threatened to choke her. Her dreams had been constant, then ceased, and now, once again, he was back and had left a note saying exactly what she wanted to hear. His message contained her name, not Maddy's. He'd never even uttered it before.

She stared at the ceiling. "Please, God, help me. I think I've lost my mind." Although she prayed, the best she could hope to get was strength to accept the truth. Joshua was a dream, and one only she could stop.

When all her tears were shed, she went into the bathroom to wash her face. No use trying to go back to sleep with so much on her mind and so little time left before work. She bent over the sink and splashed cold water on her face, then straightened and peered into the mirror. If only she could wash away the hurt and confusion as easily as the mascara streaking her cheeks, but those things were only erasable by time.

But how much time?

She needed coffee. On her way to the kitchen, passing through the bedroom, Faith gasped. Why hadn't she noticed *it* before?

She bent and picked up her hope. Holding the silken material to her nose, she inhaled Joshua's lingering scent from his red sash. Her knees weakened. She sagged onto the bed's edge. The letter hadn't been a dream. She held in her hands, proof her lover was real. A smile blossomed across her face and in her heart.

Joshua was out there somewhere, and she had only to find him. He did love her. Reminiscent of the manuscripts she read every day, Faith Oliver had found her happy ending…or perhaps the beginning. Tomorrow, she and Todd had lots to talk about.

The End

Ages of Love

HOPE HARRISON
AGE FORTY-NINE

Hope adjusted the headphone, a nervous gesture she'd developed when expecting to hear Dr. Samuelson tell a patient bad news. In his usual gravelly voice he shared the unexpected diagnosis; *terminal ovarian cancer*. How could such a horrid disease strike someone so young? She clutched her chest, removed her headset, and took a break from transcribing the medical record.

Listening to the patient's visit on tape provided a wake up call. The poor woman's medical history detailed the advanced stages of her disease with no likelihood of survival, despite recommended therapy. Hope's heart hammered, making her more aware of her need to be more proactive in her own healthcare. She hadn't seen her doctor in several years. How would she handle the discovery of such a horrific ailment?

She pushed away from her desk, stood, and walked to the kitchen in search of the phone list she kept in a drawer. She grappled through the junk, making a mental note to straighten things out, and then with the list in hand, dialed her gynecologist's number.

"Dr. Carlson's office." A chipper voice answered.

Hope held the phone away from her ear and rechecked the number she'd dialed.

"Hello? Is anyone there?"

Despite the receiver being near her shoulder, Hope heard the voice and reacted. "I...I'm sorry. She studied the number again. "I must have misdialed. I'm trying to reach Dr. Smith's Office."

"Oh, you've dialed correctly. Dr. Smith retired and transferred his practice to Dr. Jerrod Carlson. Are you calling for an appointment?"

Hope took a deep breath and gathered courage. Seeing a new doctor brought on the need to gasp in air. "I...I guess it's been longer than I thought since I last saw Doctor Smith. Yes, I do need to be seen."

There, she'd done it. Despite her previous tenure as a practicing registered nurse, she detested anything to do with her own medical issues, especially ones that involved disrobing and being probed. Did anyone really enjoy it?

She'd tried a female doctor at one time, and even a gender change didn't help. In fact, she became more self-conscious after seeing the youth of the physician, and couldn't get past wondering if the doctor was comparing her own svelte body with

Hope's older, not so shapely one.

The receptionist gave her a time and date, and Hope hung up. An image of Dr. Smith's familiar face danced through her mind. Years of seeing him had provided some semblance of comfort. Knowing he'd seen her naked countless times eased her modest pride. A smile caught her lips when she recalled the way he always warmed the speculum for her pap smear, though certainly not just for her. The added courtesy failed to lend any consolation to hearing those familiar words: 'relax and let your knees fall apart.' Now she had to face hearing them from someone she'd never met.

****

Hope's high heels clicked against the tile floor and reverberated in the emptiness as she hurried down the medical clinic's long corridor. She glanced at her watch and grimaced. Great! Late for her first appointment with a new doctor. Some first impression she'd make. The thought brought an immediate chuckle. Silly her for thinking doctors ever sat and waited for their patients.

Her moment of facetiousness faded and her palms dampened at the prospect of the ritualistic feminine torture called an annual exam. On the menu loomed the dreaded mammogram. That test had to have been developed by a man with a genuine hatred for women. Another female would never think of putting a '*sister*' through such agony. She clasped her breast in dreaded anticipation and grimaced. If only she headed toward a cabana on a Hawaiian beach instead of a cold gynecologist's table. A slight pause before entering Dr. Carlson's suite helped fortify her for the coming trial.

The unfamiliar name on the wall plaque struck an odd note. She took a deep breath, turned the knob and stopped in the doorway, her gaze locked on the packed waiting room. All eyes turned toward her, sending a warming flush up her neck. She forced a smile and crossed the ecru carpeting, wrote her name on the check-in list, and searched for an empty seat. The only one remaining was in the far corner next to the water cooler. Convenient, since the long walk from the parking lot left her feeling parched.

Hope traversed the room, avoiding the crossed and puffy feet blocking her path. Was she the only person there not pregnant? Clearly, she was the oldest. Why didn't OB/GYN doctors maintain separate waiting areas? Feeling like the lone spotted pup in a litter of black ones, she took her seat.

Within a short time, more women had signed in, and lined the wall. Rather than surrender her seat, Hope stretched across the chair's arm to fill her cup. The water soothed her dry throat but did little to quell the queasy feeling in her stomach. Despite being all too familiar with the process, the thought of going through it set her nerves on edge. She glanced at the reception door, took the last sip of water, and fought the urge to leave. After all, shouldn't she surrender her seat to an expectant mother? She offered, but sadly no one accepted.

The trash receptacle sat about six feet away. Not eager to become the object of unwanted stares again, she wadded the pleated paper into a ball and risked a rim shot at the can. Luckily, the cup teetered on the wastebasket's edge and then fell inside. Another woman watched from the other side of the room. Hope, her cheeks warm, shrugged her shoulders and flashed a grin before she hid her face behind a magazine. She absentmindedly thumbed through the pages, but her gaze wandered to the swollen belly of the young lady seated next to her.

A pang of sadness stabbed at Hope's heart. The girl probably had a husband...and a home that would soon house a complete family. Thoughts of Alan, her beloved husband, taken three years ago in an auto accident, blurred Hope's vision. Although she'd prayed for children for years, they'd never been able to conceive. Evidently, God had ignored her pleas.

At forty-nine and a widow, the parent ship sailed long ago. The only baby in her life was Chloe, her Maltese puppy. Hope blew an upward stream to air to dry her misting eyes and then surveyed the remaining crowd. More pregnant bellies only made her sadder. She returned to her magazine and settled in for a long wait.

The reception window opened with a squeal reminiscent of fingernails on a blackboard. Hope shivered and flashed back to grammar school—an amazing recollection given the time passed.

"Hope Harrison?" A woman behind the glass called.

Hope nearly sprinted to the window. "That's me."

The gray-haired receptionist handed her a clipboard. "I need you to fill this out since you're a new patient. We need to update your file."

"But…but I'm not new, the doctor is."

The older woman clearly forced a smile. "Well, dear, you're new to the doctor, so please complete both sides."

Hope accepted the form and turned in time to see someone claim her seat. Great. No one wanted it when she offered, but now that her feet hurt from being stuffed into pretentious shoes she never should have worn, she stood.

She glanced around the room, counting patients. How many did this doctor see in a day? The wait would take forever. She'd found the perfect excuse to reschedule. Stacks of tapes at home needed transcribing and her feet hurt like hell. She'd just convinced herself to take flight when a nurse appeared in the doorway and summoned her.

Hope's eyes widened. How could it be her turn already? She'd been one of the last to arrive. "But I haven't completed my forms yet." She waived the clipboard at the woman in white.

"No problem. Follow me and you can finish in the exam room."

They stopped first at the scale. Hope grimaced, but stepped on and closed her eyes. Her efforts to remain in the dark were for naught when the nurse announced her weight of one-forty loud enough for anyone in the vicinity to hear. Hope's cheeks warmed, but at least she knew why her clothes felt tighter of late. She'd gained fifteen pounds since the last time she'd weighed. When had that been?

The nurse motioned her toward an open door.

Hope sat in the lone chair and completed the monotonous paperwork. The draped exam table, waiting stirrups and gown acted like a magnet and drew her gaze. Dread gnawed at her. She still had time to leave, and although fleeing was a preferable choice, running away wasn't an option. She wasn't the only woman in the world who endured the impending procedures. Besides, what could possibly be worse than finding out she wasn't one-hundred-twenty-five pounds anymore? She weighed that since her wedding.

Visions of Jenny Craig and NutriSystem flashed through her mind.

"Be brave," she whispered to her childish self…the part of her that truly wanted to run like the wind out of the exam room.

Standing, she placed her completed forms on the counter next to the small stainless-steel sink. How many times had she washed her hands in one just like it? But, that was another life and time. Her nursing career ended with Alan's death.

"I need to get your vitals."

The voice caused Hope to jump. She climbed up on the edge of the table, and offered her left arm.

The nurse recorded blood pressure and temperature in a chart and then thrust the paper gown at Hope. "Remove all your clothing and put this on. The doctor will be with you shortly." She left, closing the door behind her. Had Hope's nursing persona been so devoid of warmth.

Unfortunately, she knew the drill. Leave the opening in front for the breast exam and cover with the drape. Hope flicked open the flimsy blue plastic, shook it out to its full length and stretched it across the exam table. How many times had she laid out an identical one for a patient? Funny, she'd forgotten how small they were.

She sighed and kicked off her heels, wiggled her toes and vowed never to put her feet into anything other than flats. "Ah, what a relief." Her voice echoed in the empty room.

Despite nervous fingers working against her, she unfastened the small buttons on her blouse, shrugged out of it, and hung it on the back of the chair. She unzipped her skirt and shimmied out of it to a bawdy tune in her head, urging her to *take it all off*. Certainly, her laughter sounded in the hallway. Who in their right mind would pay her to strip? No one she knew, and the thought saddened her for a moment…until she recalled how Alan always lit up when she undressed for him. Still, those fifteen added pounds haunted her.

She draped her skirt atop her blouse, then perched on the edge of the chair and peeled off her panty hose. Why in the world she'd gone to the trouble to dress up remained a mystery. She should have just worn the comfy sweats she spent the majority of her time wearing. Of course, that was a perk of working from home.

Maybe she gussied up today because her social life died along with her husband, and she had a closet full of clothes crying to be worn. Yeah, that was the reason. Any outing provided a chance to veer from the norm.

"I'm pathetic," she muttered, and stripped off her black panties and bra. She put her undergarments over her shoes and tucked them under the chair. Her love for sexy lingerie in no way made her an exhibitionist. Wearing black was a habit she'd acquired to please her husband, and she wasn't ready for granny panties yet.

She stood in the nude, goose bumps peppering her skin. Was it really necessary to keep the examining rooms so cold? Of course, the reason was to avoid contagious germs, but any left from a previous patient had long ago died of frostbite.

Hope donned the gown, clutched the ends together and then climbed up on the table again. As before, the paper crinkled and stuck to her skin. She exhaled a pent-up breath and told herself this would all be over in a short time—sort of like a prisoner waiting for a lethal injection. Being the person to hand out the gown was quite different from being the one wearing it. No wonder she'd avoided seeing the doctor for so long.

Crossing and uncrossing her ankles, Hope tried to find a comfortable position. The blood supply to her feet became stilted by the bend of her knees pressing against the table's edge and her legs dangling midair. Within a few moments, her toes turned numb. She was about to step down when footsteps paused outside and someone rapped on the door.

"Come in." That really wasn't what she wanted to say.

"Ms. Harrison?" A deep, resonating voice

preceded the doctor into the room.

He walked into the examination room, and Hope's breath hitched. The man was the epitome of Adonis—dark hair, with just a touch of grey at the temples, a Tom Selleck moustache, and eyes identical to Paul Newman's. Where was ol' Doc Carson, the senior citizen of a man she'd imagined had taken over Dr. Smith's practice?

"Hello. I'm pleased to meet you Ms. Harrison. I'm Dr. Carlson." He flipped open her chart. "I see you've been a patient of Dr. Smith's for a number of years."

Where was her voice? Clearly, this was her new physician, and she found herself dumbstruck. "Y...yes, I started coming to Doctor Smith when I was just a teenager. I was surprised to hear he'd retired."

Dr. Carlson cocked his head. "Where have you been? He's been gone for over a year."

A warming flush crept up her heck. I'll fess up. I've been preoccupied with my new home business and haven't had time to make an appointment...but, I'm here now."

"So you are. I'll call my assistant in and we can get started."

Hope's heartbeat jumped up a few notches, and she chewed her bottom lip. Being subjected to the indignity that lay ahead didn't appeal to her, but then she doubted the doctor enjoyed the core either. The tedium of seeing so many patients in one day had been tiring for her, so she imagined seeing body after body, day after day, grew old for the physician, too.

Dr. Carlson depressed a green button on the wall and his nurse appeared like magic. He avoided making eye contact with Hope and focused on the woman in colorful scrubs. "Will you please get Ms. Harrison into position for her pap and breast exam?"

Hope took a deep breath and reclined. She inched her feet around, searching for the metal stirrups and finally found them. Without being told, Hope slid all the way to the bottom of the table. The provided drape seemed the size of a postage stamp.

Dr. Carlson stood at the counter, donning his disposable gloves. Hope's stomach rumbled—a loud, gurgling growl like she hadn't eaten in weeks. The doctor turned and smiled. He'd heard it. After all, he wasn't nearly deaf like her old doctor.

Hope pressed on her abdomen to quell the noise, certain her cheeks were bright red. She turned her head to the doctor. "It's been quite a while since I've assumed this position, and I think my stomach is protesting." Her comment sounded corny, but better than the awkward silence that issued an invitation for her guts to grumble again.

The doctor perched on the rolling stool. "I expect you'll find there's been no change in the exam procedure since your last visit, so let's get it over with, shall we?" He disappeared beyond the drape. "Just let your knees fall apart."

She rolled her eyes. Easy for him to say, and with a deep breath, she willed her legs to go limp. The cold edge of the speculum touched her nether region and she jumped.

He patted her knee. "Sorry. Relax for me."

The more he asked her to relax, the less relaxed she became. She counted holes in the acoustic ceiling tiles while grimacing at the pinching pain. He palpated her ovaries and she groaned. Dr. Carlson might look a darn sight better than her previous doc but he sure didn't have the same gentle touch.

"There. All done." Dr. Carlson stood and peeled off his gloves and threw them in the waste can.

Without warning, he stepped to the side of the table and bared her breast. She went back to counting holes while he kneaded her boob like a baker preparing dough. She kept her gaze focused on the ceiling until he finished and covered her again.

"Well, Hope, everything appears to be fine, but I'll need to get the results of your pap and the films from your mammogram. You are scheduled to have one today, aren't you?"

Yes, she had a ticket for the vice grip from hell. She nodded.

"Good, I'll step out and let you get dressed. When you're ready, my office is right across the hall.

Please come in and have a seat and I'll be with you as soon as I finish with the patient next door. He turned and left, his nurse followed.

Hope had never seen eyes so blue…and such a strong jaw. She grasped the drape to her chest, hoping to quell the flutterings of her heart. Last time she'd felt this way, she'd been a schoolgirl.

She obviously needed to get out more, if seeing a handsome man affected her so. She slid off the table and checked her wristwatch. Still an hour before her mammogram, she scrambled into her clothes, discarded the gown, and took a minute to poof up the flat spot in the back of her hair. Slinging her purse over her shoulder, she strolled across the hall, glad to escape the claustrophobic exam room. A lack of windows always made it hard for her to breathe.

Hope stopped in the doorway of the doctor's office and eyed the framed diplomas hanging behind his mahogany desk. He had quite an impressive background, but what she searched for were pictures of a wife and children. She saw none.

Taking a seat in one of two leather armchairs, she attempted to appear at ease. Nerves still tingled through her, so she went through the crossing and uncrossing ritual of her ankles to find a comfortable position. She smoothed the front of her blouse, tucked her shoulder-length hair behind her ears, and then reached into her purse for her compact. Even at home, fresh lipstick was a must.

She grinned into the small mirror, checking her teeth for stains and caught sight of Dr. Carlson's reflection. She snapped the oval compact shut and jammed it back into her purse but not before noticing the redness in her cheeks.

"Sorry about the wait." He walked behind his desk, sat, then flipped through her chart. A hint of a smile showed on his face, but he quickly sobered when he glanced up. "I don't see any current medications in your records. Dr. Smith prescribed Valium for you some time ago, but that's all I'm seeing in his notes."

"I'm not taking anything at the present time. Dr. Smith gave me that medicine to help me deal with the death of my husband." Her shoulders tensed at the memory.

Dr. Carlson's brow creased. "Oh, I'm…I'm so sorry for your loss."

"Thank you, but I'm doing fine. My Alan died almost three years ago and like they say, time heals all wounds." What *they* say was a lie. She still missed her husband so much she often cried herself to sleep. Just thinking of him misted her eyes. She blinked back tears.

"So, you aren't taking any prescribed meds at this time?"

"No," She uncrossed her ankles.

"Anything over the counter?"

"No." She crossed her legs and tugged at her hem so as not to expose too much.

"Do you have any medical issues you'd like to discuss with me?"

She shook her head. "Other than being tired on occasion, I feel pretty good most of the time."

"No hot flashes or night sweats?"

What was he insinuating? She planted her feet firmly on the floor. "None to speak of." Her tone held a trace of iciness.

"Mood swings?"

Hope leaned forward. "Dr. Carlson, why don't you just ask me if I think I'm experiencing menopause? I was a nurse so I know all the symptoms."

He jerked back in his chair. "I...I didn't mean to insult you. Your blood pressure concerns me. It's higher than normal, and sometimes—"

"I had my last period a year ago." She took a deep breath and leaned back. "I lied about the flashes and sweating, and have both, but I refuse to take hormone replacement therapy because of the cancer risk. I'm sure my blood pressure is high because of stress. I've been trying to establish a home business, and—"

"I guess I should have read your chart more closely. I hadn't noticed you're a nurse."

"Was...not anymore." She stared into her lap, her shoulders tense from confessing her lies.

"Sad. We've such a shortage of qualified people in the field. Do you mind if I ask why you left nursing?"

She looked up and shrugged. "It's no secret. My husband died from injuries sustained in an automobile accident. He lingered for three weeks while I sat by, helpless and unable to ease his suffering. I realize people die every day, but watching him deteriorate went against the oath I took when I entered nursing. After he passed, I didn't have the desire to continue in the profession."

The doctor's Adam's apple bobbed with a hard swallow. "I'm sorry to bring up such a painful topic for you." He pulled a prescription pad from his desk drawer and quickly scribbled his signature. When finished, he tore the paper free and handed it across the desk. "This medication has nothing to do with menopause and carries no cancer risks we know of."

Hope hesitated to accept the prescription and leaned further back.

He waggled the paper at her. "As someone schooled in medicine, you must realize ignoring issues that can affect your heart health is foolhardy. This medication will merely regulate your blood pressure, nothing more. I recommend you take the pills as directed, and I'd like to see you again in a month. By that time, I'll have the results of your tests and also get a good idea of how this medicine is working for you. Do you have any questions?"

She signed and reached for the paper. "None that come to mind." She focused on the scenery beyond the window behind him. Of course, she had a million questions, but none that seemed appropriate for the moment.

He stood, drawing her attention to him. "If you think of anything, feel free to call the office." He extended his hand. "It was very nice to meet you."

Hope rose and shook hands with him. Warmth spread up her arm and radiated into her chest. His eyes bored into her very soul, but she chalked that part up to an over-imagination.

While holding his right hand, she made a cursory inspection of his left. He wore no wedding ring, but then lots of men didn't. The lack of a tan line gave her a rush of hope. She flashed a smile and released her grasp. "Thank you. I'll see you next month...and I will take the medication."

She walked toward the exit, pausing at the reception desk to make a return appointment before heading for her next stop. After meeting her new doctor, having a Mammogram didn't seem like such a big deal. The test results provided her with a reason to return.

Instead of worrying about her blood pressure and breast health, why couldn't she get his sexy image out of her mind? How old was he? Age was such a hard thing to judge, especially in men. Hardly fair for him to know about her night sweats and hot flashes, and she only knew his name, what colleges he attended and that he didn't wear a wedding ring. Did it matter? He'd shown no interest in her other than as a patient, so why act like a teenager, hoping for a date to the prom? Surely, a conflict of interest rule dictated socialization between a doctor and patient. Unfortunately, nothing conflicted with her interest in him.

She passed through an almost empty waiting room on her way out. Only two pregnant women remained, chatting, laughing, and comparing bellies. If only Alan had left her with a child, she wouldn't be alone. The cliché, *no use crying over spilled milk* ran though her mind as she closed the door behind her and made her way back down the long corridor. The door marked *Radiology* might as well have said *gallows* because by the time she arrived there, an invisible noose tightened around her neck and drained the moisture from her mouth. So much for finding a good reason for torture.

She splayed her fingers across her chest. "I'm sorry for what I'm about to put you girls through, but I have no choice. Doctor's orders."

****

With Chloe nestled at her feet, Hope settled back at her desk and breathed a sigh of relief at having her annual exam behind her. Of course, she still had to wait for the test results before really relaxing, but she'd get to see Doctor Carlson again, and that definitely was a plus. Hopefully, there would be no unpleasant surprises—health or otherwise.

She adjusted her headphones and reach over to push the start button on the recorder, but paused. Visions of her doctor ran through her mind. Those eyes, trim body, the slight dimples when he smiled...all qualities guaranteed to make a nun considering changing her faith. At least Hope would, except she wasn't Catholic.

Something about the man drew her like a magnet. Maybe she'd gone without sex for far too long. No, that wasn't it. Even if she'd been intimate ten minutes before seeing him, she'd still be attracted.

The stack of tapes on her desk beckoned. She pushed thoughts of Dr. C from her mind and set her fingertips flying on the keyboard and listened to the usual array of maladies—everything from an infected hangnail to a boil in need of lancing. Listening to assessments of others' problems rather than worrying about her own was much more pleasant.

She was in the middle of transcribing notes about a urinary tract infection when the phone rang. She didn't recognize the number on her caller ID and decided to let the machine pick up the call. Someone from the pharmacy announced her prescription was ready. Although she detested taking medication, the little pill the doctor prescribed was her ticket to see his handsome face again. She finished the tape she worked on, ran a brush through her hair and headed to Wexler's drugstore.

****

"Honestly?" Sandy's eyes widened at Hope's description of Dr. Carlson. "My doctor's older than dirt." Her neighbor shook her head and faked a shiver. "I'm not sure I'd feel comfortable undressing in front of someone so yummy." She rose from the kitchen table, went back to the counter, and returned with the coffee pot. "More?"

Hope pushed her cup toward Sandy. "Half please. Your stuff is too high octane for me. I wanna sleep tonight so I'll look my best for my appointment tomorrow." She chuckled.

Sandy had been the first to welcome Alan and Hope to the neighborhood when they moved into their new home. The two women had struck up an immediate friendship and had been like sisters ever since.

"Do I detect a note of interest in your voice?" Sandy shot Hope a perplexed look. "Those brown eyes of yours sparkle whenever you mention your new doc."

Hope flicked her wrist. "For heaven's sake, he's probably married and has a passel of kids. Leave me to my dreams." She heaved a sigh. "Besides, he barely noticed me. I'm just another chart as far as he's concerned."

"Oh, I think you're forgetting you're an attractive woman, Hope. Give yourself some credit. The man would have to be blind not to notice a leggy brunette, and I'm sure he did." Never one to disappoint, Sandy always built up Hope's ego. "Still, he's a professional, and I'm sure you wouldn't feel very comfortable if he shot goo-goo eyes at you."

"Goo-goo eyes? Where did that come from?"

Sandy grinned. "I have no idea, but you know what I mean."

"I get it, but I'd settle for a simple hint that he was interested in me."

Sandy poured herself another cup of coffee and then returned to her seat. "You do realize this is the first time you've shown an interest in another man since—"

"I know, and feeling emotions again is strange...like I'm betraying Alan's memory."

"That's silly. You've mourned Alan long enough. Besides, he'd want you to be happy."

Hope downed the last of her coffee and dabbed a napkin to her lips. "I thought I was happy until I saw Dr. Carlson and went all giddy. He may have controlled my blood pressure with his magic little pills, but I doubt he can give me anything to get thoughts of him out of my brain. I may have to change doctors."

Sandy's brow furrowed. "Before you do something so drastic, give the good doc a dose of Hope. It might be just what he needs."

Hope rolled her eyes as she stood. "A dose? My, aren't we getting medical? If I plan to follow your suggestion, I'd best get home and find my prescription pad. Gotta dash."

****

The waiting room wasn't nearly as crowded as the last time. Hope signed in, found a vacant chair and took a seat. At the thought of seeing her handsome doctor again, her palms dampened. Probably a waste of perspiration since doctors didn't date their patients, and he was most likely married.

"Ms. Harrison?" The same nurse as before appeared in the doorway.

"Yes, I'm here." Hope stood, her stomach churning, and followed the woman down the familiar hallway. She'd given little thought to her test results, so feasting her eyes on the doctor again had to be the cause. A stop at the scales dampened her excitement, especially finding out she'd put on two pounds since the last weigh-in. She didn't even ask about her blood pressure measurements, just pouted that seventeen pounds had turned to nineteen and might soon be twenty-five if she didn't do something. How could she have gained in only a month? Maybe she'd removed her shoes at the scales last time, but she didn't think so. She grimaced at the thought of switching from sweats to muu-muus to hide developing rolls. Trailing behind the nurse, Hope craned her neck trying to catch a glimpse of her own behind. Did she look as fat as she felt?

"Dr. Carson asked me to seat you in his office instead of a room to go over your test results." The nurse turned and caught Hope in a contorted position. She straightened, and offered no explanation for her bizarre actions. What could she possibly say?

"Fine." Despite heat creeping into her cheeks, Hope flashed a smile and sagged into the same chair she'd sat in before. Her mind still boggled at the increase in her weight. Why hadn't she noticed?

Her gaze wandered the doctor's office, appreciating the seascape to the left and the tidiness of his desk. She focused on a stack of patient files and recalled the young woman who'd received devastating news from her physician. The possibility of a negative outcome hit her like a bag of bricks. How would she react to bad news? She swallowed hard and summoned positive thoughts. Death by disease or obesity, which would be worse?

"Ms. Harrison, how nice to see you again." Dr. Carlson appeared in the doorway, walked closer and offered his hand.

Her concerns faded as she eyed his open white lab coat and the powder blue shirt beneath. A vee of tanned skin matted with dark hair caught her gaze, until she realized she stared. "N...nice to see you, too." She clasped palms with him in a brief shake.

He peered down his perfectly formed nose. "I have some good news for you. Your blood pressure is much lower today, your mammogram is normal, and your pap test came back negative for any problems."

Hope expelled a breath. "That's a relief."

He smiled, walked to his chair, and sat. "I'm pleased the medication I prescribed worked for you."

"Me, too, although I wasn't aware I had a problem"

"That's why high BP is called 'the silent killer'."

She stared into her lap. "I guess I'd forgotten that. You'd think I'd be more mindful since I transcribe medical records daily."

"You're a transcriptionist now?"

As much as she wanted to avoid his captivating eyes, she looked up. "The new business I mentioned before. After my husband passed, I decided to try something new. My medical background provided the perfect opportunity to transfer doctor's notes into charts. I have to say my job is much easier than reading the handwriting I dealt with through the years."

He closed her chart and leaned back. "I confess. My writing is illegible even when I try to be neat." Dr. Carlson picked up his pen and twirled it midair, like a baton. "How many doctors use your services?"

She held back a smile at his question. "I *transcribe* for three at the moment, but I'd like to expand to five."

"Really?" He stopped fidgeting with his pen. "I'm in the market for someone to do my transcription. Would you consider taking me on as a client? His blue eyes sparkled.

She'd done nothing but consider taking him on since she first saw him, but not as a client. Still, he didn't need to know that. A smile blossomed on her lips. "Sure...of course. I'd be pleased to work for you, but don't you want to know my fee first?"

"I'm sure it's competitive, but..." He sat forward and rested his elbows on his desk.

Her mind spun under his scrutiny. Instead of money, she wanted to discuss his marital status, but how did one slip that question in a conversation?

"Well, are you going to tell me or not?" He probed with a smile.

"Oh, yes. I charge nine cents per line. I'm also very dependable and fast." Oh crap, she thought. Why hadn't she said quick instead?

He lowered one eye in a wink. "I'm very

interested. I'd love to give you a try."

Okay, was he toying with her or referring to business? Two could play this game. "When would you like to start?" She crossed her legs, feeling totally at ease with their exchange."

"How about tomorrow?" He mimicked her posture.

She crossed her arms. "Fine, what do you propose?" Her heart thudded as it had the first time she saw him.

"I'll gather my tapes together and deliver them to your house around seven, if that's okay." He rested crossed arms on the desk.

"Seven..." Her breath hitched. He was coming to her house? "I'll be there. Do you need directions?"

"No, I have your address and G.P.S., so I think I can figure out how to get there."

"I have no doubt." An urge to slap herself upside the head grew. Why was she turning everything he said into a sexual innuendo? What was wrong with her? He was her doctor, for heaven's sake, and they were only discussing a business venture. Still hadn't he put an emphasis on a few key words...and what about that wink?

The doctor stood. "I'd love to chat more, but I have other patients waiting. I'll see you tomorrow evening, then." He offered his hand again.

His professional farewell caused the aura of

sexual tension to drop like a lead balloon. Hope's spirit dampened, but she clasped hands with him, hoping to hide her disappointment. "Yes, tomorrow, then."

****

Hope glanced down at the clock in the corner of her computer screen; already six o'clock, and she expected Dr. Carlson at seven. She'd been totally lost in transcribing and lost track of time. Pushing back from her desk, she pondered changing out of her gray sweats into something more impressive, but then shook her head. "For what?"

Clearly, he was coming over to drop off his files and nothing more. He'd probably be in a hurry to get home to his wife and kids, so why go to the trouble of dressing up for ten minutes? The phone interrupted her thoughts.

"Are you nervous? What are you wearing? Did you remember to daub a little cologne on your pulse spots?" Sandy barely ended one question before tossing out another.

"Slow down, woman. This isn't a date."

"I know, I know. Still, you want to make a good impression."

"The man has seen me naked and fondled my breasts. I sort of think it's a little late for first impressions. Besides, I dressed up for my appointment and by the time he came in the room, everything I wore was hanging on a chair or stuffed in my shoes. He had his chance."

Sandy chuckled. "Then this is your chance. You'll be kicking yourself if you don't look your best. I know you."

Hope fell silent for a moment. "Okay, you win. I'll change into something totally fake and unrealistic. There's nothing like creating a false image to win over a man...but I tell you he's probably married." She glimpsed the clock on the wall. "If I'm going to make an amazing transformation, I've gotta go. I'll call you the minute he leaves."

"Don't forget. I can't wait to hear what happens."

Hope dashed into the bathroom and turned on the shower. Clothing options played in her mind while the water warmed. Something casual yet sexy. Did she even have anything fitting that description?

After she showered and dried off, she wrapped herself in her towel and stood in her walk-in closet, staring at her wardrobe. Some of the clothes hadn't been worn in years, and some probably no longer fit. She selected black slacks and a lightweight ivory sweater with a dropped neckline. The air conditioning still ran most of the time even though it was early August. "Hmm," she muttered while studying her top. "Push up bra, better posture...and cleavage. May as well."

Once she'd dressed, she pulled a brush through the simple cut. A poof here, a spray there, and she smiled. A soft perm kept styling manageable and gave her hair the body it lacked. Only she and the checker at Walmart knew her true color.

Hope turned from one-side to the other in front of the mirror. "Not bad for an old broad. I've seen worse." She eyed her rear-end. "And, my butt isn't nearly as big as I feared."

Her mumbling drew Chloe, who appeared from the bedroom and bounced around, wanting attention.

"No baby. I'm not picking you up. Dog hair and black pants don't go well together." She reached down and patted the pup on the head, then straightened and nabbed her special 'Jessica" cologne. With Sandy's voice ringing in her hears, Hope applied a spray behind each ear and in the hollow of her throat. "Forget the back of the knees," she muttered. "Fat chance I'll need it there."

Showered, groomed and perfumed, she'd gone to a lot of trouble for a man who might be married. She stood over Chloe, her hands on her hips. "Somehow asking Doctor Carlson about his marital status is a difficult question to fit into a conversation. What if I say, I charge nine cents a line...oh, and by the way, are you married?" She laughed and shook her head. "No, Chlo...that wouldn't work. What about, my husband has been gone for three years...how about your wife? She still around?" Chloe cocked her heard and eyed her mistress before she trotted to the rug and nestled at the foot of the bed.

"Fine...don't help me, then." Hope chuckled under her breath. "When the time is right, that hunk of burning love will mention something that'll clarify everything. You just wait and see."

A melodic chime set the dog barking. "Hush, Chloe. Be a good girl." Hope made her way to the living room and opened the door. She stiffened her jaw to keep it from going slack and swallowed hard. Doctor Carlson's smile stole her breath.

Her faux sedate gaze traveled the length of him, taking in his black polo shirt, muscle-hugging Levis and white tennis shoes that looked as though he'd recently taking them out of the box they came in. The man looked even better out of his lab coat that didn't do his broad shoulders justice. She swallowed again. "Hi...please come in." *Said the spider to the fly*, played in her head and completed her thought.

He stepped inside, a brown bag under his arm. "Good evening, Hope." He paused and smiled. "May I call you Hope?"

Rather than lean against the open door for support, she closed it. "Oh...of course, and please, have a seat." She gestured to the sofa.

He sat, relaxed against the cushioned back, but

his eyes widened when Chloe sprang into his lap and licked his face. Hope snatched up the dog. "I'm so sorry, Doctor Carlson. This is Chloe, and as you can see, she's very friendly."

"Yes, she certainly is," he said wiping his chin. "I love dogs, she just caught me off guard...and, if I'm going to address you by your first name, you have to call me Jerrod."

Hope bent and placed Chloe on the floor and, with a little smack on her behind, sending the pup scurrying out of the room. Hope straightened and smiled at the doctor. "Can I get you something to drink?"

Jerrod held out the crinkled brown paper bag. First, here's the tapes I need transcribed. I apologize for the container, but it's the best I could find on short notice."

"Whatever works is my motto." She accepted his offering, stepped through an archway into her office, placed the bag on her desk, and then returned. "Now, can I get you something?"

"Do you have a beer?"

Why hadn't she bought a six-pack? She flashed an exaggerated frown. "I'm sorry, I don't. I have Diet Pepsi, Diet Seven-up, iced tea, or I can make a pot of coffee."

"Iced tea sounds good."

"Sweet or not?" Hope asked.

"I'm beginning to feel like I'm in a restaurant." He chuckled. "Sweet please."

"Be right back." In the kitchen, Hope clung to the cabinet to steel her wobbly legs. She'd expected him to toss the tapes at her and leave, but he didn't. Doctor Carlson sat on her couch, just a few feet away, awaiting his drink, and he'd asked her to call him Jerrod. Despite being overcome by her good fortune, she retrieved a pitcher of tea from the fridge, poured two glassfuls over ice, stirred sugar into one, and returned with them to the living room. "Here you go."

He sat with knees apart and one arm resting along the back of her sofa. She longed to cozy up next to him, but he used two hands to accept the drink, flashing his trademark smile. "Thanks." He eyed the tea but didn't mention the unsettled sugar whirling around inside as he placed the glass on a coaster on the side table.

She sat next to him, and avoiding eye contact that cried out for conversation, fixed her gaze on the enticing bulge in the crotch of his jeans. She yanked her chin upward, her mouth void of moisture and heat creeping up her neck. What possessed her to act so strange?

The moment he reached for his tea, she inched toward the opposite end of the couch to access the end table, and placed her drink there, then curled her legs around her bottom. The room grew far too warm and she resisted the urge to fan herself.

He took a sip. "Very good."

"Thank you. It's sun tea." She raised her own glass to her lips.

An awkward silence ensued.

He swiveled to face her. "Do I make you uncomfortable?"

"Yes—no. Okay, I lied." She put her tea down and twisted her fingers together. "Yes, I feel a tad uncomfortable, but only because it's been such a long time since I've had a gentleman visit."

"Would I make you feel better if I told you I'm not always a gentleman?" His deep chuckle peppered her clammy skin with goose bumps.

His flirtatious nature came as an extra bonus to his visit, but she couldn't reciprocate without knowing an important answer. Curiosity ate at her. She had to find a polite way to ask.

"Are you married?" The words tumbled out before she realized she'd spoke them.

He showed no surprise. "I was...once."

"Was?" A smile threatened, but she remained stoic.

"Yes, I've been divorced for a number of years. My ex couldn't handle being married to a doctor, but then, I'm sure you understand the time demands...especially since you've been part of the healthcare profession."

A pent-up breath escaped her. "Of course. My late husband didn't appreciate all the nights I worked in the ER, but he understood that shift work came with the credentials until one gained some seniority." Muscles that earlier tensed, relaxed. Her handsome doctor wasn't married, after all.

A stifled smile now blossomed with her newfound information.

He twined and untwined his fingers. "I...I like you, Hope." He stared at the floor. "I have from the moment I met you in the exam room." He glanced up, his blue eyes narrowing. "Your humor is refreshing and we share something in common. I haven't found that in a long time."

She widened her eyes. "I feel the same about you." She did, but it wasn't his sense of humor that hooked her at first glance and... he hadn't even mentioned if he found her looks appealing. Didn't he know that bit of knowledge was important to a woman? Maybe if she fished a little, she might learn more. Hope picked up her tea and ran a finger around the glass rim. "I'm quite surprised someone with your good looks hasn't been already snapped up." She took a sip.

"I could say the same about you. You're quite beautiful."

Her bait attracted the very response she sought. She lowered her gaze. "Thank you. It's been ages since someone paid me such a compliment. I'm not sure how to react."

Jerrod inched closer, then closer, until the heat from his biceps filtered through her sweater and sent a jolt down her arm. He grasped her hand. "I'm not sure how to act, either, but I know I've wanted to do this since I first saw you. Please don't think me bold."

He snaked an arm behind her and pulled her close. The silent moment filled with magic, and her breath hitched when he covered her mouth with his and sought entrance with his probing tongue. The sweet taste of tea lingered on his lips.

****

Hope arched away and peered into his eyes. Her head still rested on his firm biceps, and his enticing aftershave wafted around her. Taking a minute to compose herself, she touched her lips and sighed. "Wow, I never expected that."

His throat rippled with a swallow. "You didn't find it offensive did you? I couldn't help myself."

"I said I didn't expect it, not, I didn't welcome it." She touched the back of his hand. "I've wondered for over a month what kissing you would be like, and that was everything I imagined. Besides, we're not in high school anymore; we're grown adults who know what we want and need."

Jerrod stared into his lap and picked at the hem of his shirt. "So, where do we go from here? A doctor dating a patient is more than a little unconventional, but I'm willing to give it a try if you are."

"Are you kidding me? Just ask me out and see how quickly I accept." Happiness bubbled inside her. Sitting crossed-legged, she turned her face to him. "Pinch me. I think I'm dreaming."

His gaze met hers. "I'm afraid I'll bruise that beautiful skin, but as long as I know you're walking into this relationship with eyes wide open, I'm satisfied."

She untangled her feet and wrapped her arms around his neck. "Oh, these peepers have never been wider than they are this moment."

He leaned away. "Oh, by the way, that fragrance you're wearing is quite sensual. I blame it for my boldness." He laughed and then reeled her in for another sniff.

She arched her neck and allowed him to rain butterfly kisses along her throat. "Remind me to call my friend, Sandy, and thank her."

Jerrod broke their embrace and looked at her from beneath raised brows.

She shook her head and smiled. "It's a long story, but the perfume was her idea. I didn't even expect you to walk through the door."

His brow relaxed and he turned sober. "Maybe you shouldn't have let me in, because I'm in no hurry to leave. I want to know everything there is to know about Hope Harrison."

"Then ask me anything. My life is an open book, and I hope to add another chapter after tonight."

****

Hope closed the door and leaned against it, still breathless from Jerrod's goodnight kiss. The clock on the mantle showed almost two a.m.; where had the time gone? They'd spent hours talking about anything and everything. Earlier in the day, she'd wondered if he was married, and now she knew all about him.

She itched to call her friend and share the news, but the hour was far too late. Besides, morning wasn't far off. Hope made her way to the bedroom with a permanent smile etched on her face. Dreams of Jerrod waited, and she was eager for sleep.

An annoying thought niggled at her while she changed into her pajamas. Had she been too willing and accessible? Should she have held him at arm's length and made him wait longer before they shared a kiss? Surely, dating rules had changed over the years.

She went into the bathroom and performed her nightly face-cleaning ritual in front of the mirror. Concerned eyes reflected back at her. Times had changed regarding dating . . . and she wasn't exactly sure how to act . . . it had been so long. Rule books didn't exist so she'd have to trust her gut feelings about Jerrod. Right now, her whole body still tingled from his closeness, and against her teachings of good morality, she regretted not inviting him to stay the night. "We're consenting adults, after all," she said, her lips pursed to avoid contact with the astringent pad.

****

The morning sun streamed through the blinds Hope had forgotten to close. From the angle of the orange sphere in the sky, the hour was early. Hadn't she just dozed off? One of the perks of working at home was not answering an alarm clock, but immediate thoughts of Jerrod sent her mind reeling and wiped away her sleepiness.

She rolled away from the sun's harsh glare, stretched her arms over her head and languished beneath the covers. What was her handsome doctor doing right now? Was he already at work? On his way? Was he thinking of her? Last night turned out far too good to be true. If his manly scent didn't still linger, she'd believe everything had been nothing more than a dream.

A tingle of excitement shot through her. "Oh, thank you, God. Even more, thank you Dr. Smith for retiring." She crushed an extra pillow to her chest and pictured Jarrod's handsome face.

Chloe stood next to the bed, her head cocked and eyes fixed on her owner. Hope reached down and patted her loving companion's head. "Okay, girl, breakfast coming right up."

Despite being her own boss, work beckoned. No transcription, no money, and now she had Jerrod's tapes to transcribe. She rose, straightened her bed, and plodded to the bathroom. How in the world could she concentrate on medical tapes when she couldn't keep him out of her mind? She showered quickly. If he phoned, she didn't want to miss his call.

Wrapped in a towel, she went back to the bedroom to get dressed. Her gaze wandered to her dresser and rested on the picture in the filigreed frame—her and Alan on their wedding day. She gulped down the hurtful remembrance of their happy life together and struggled with an onset of guilt. Was she being unfair to her husband's memory?

She sat on the edge of the bed and picked up the phone from the nightstand. Sandy answered after only one ring. "What in the blazes took you so long? I'm dying over here, waiting for a full report on your evening with what's his name."

"Hi, Sandy, I'm supposing you knew it was me from caller ID." Hope chucked. "Calm down, I didn't call because Jerrod left so late, I didn't think it fair to disturb your sleep."

"Okay, okay, I get it. So dish already. What

happened?"

"Nothing earth shattering. We talked a lot. He isn't married like I feared–was once, but divorced. He has no children, and most importantly, he likes me." Hope couldn't contain the inflection in her voice.

"Honestly, Hope, you're such a ditz. How can you be surprised when a man finds you attractive?" She didn't even pause for an answer. "Never mind, what else happened?"

"Take a breath. You sound like a fan who missed the Friday cliffhanger in a favorite soap opera. Jerrod and I didn't really get acquainted until last night. What did you expect to happen?"

"Sue me, I was hoping for a little more than talking." She giggled. "I have to live vicariously through someone else, you know."

"Okay, so we kissed."

"You didn't." It wasn't a question as much as an exclamation.

"Yes, and he kisses like no one else. I still can't believe he . . . pulled me into his arms and just kissed me."

"Do tell."

"Hope's declaration refreshed her guilt and the real reason she'd called in the first place. "I need your opinion, Sandy."

"About kissing?"

"No, silly. Am I being unfaithful to Alan? Am I

considering involvement with someone else too soon?" She stared at her wedding picture through misty eyes.

"I thought we already had this conversation. Do you think Alan would remain celibate forever because he once loved a wife who passed away? Trust me. He'd understand and want you to be happy. You're not cheating, for heaven's sake. It's time for you to have a life again. I hate to be cliché, but grab the brass ring while it's dangling in front of you or you'll regret missing out on the prize."

Hope sighed. "I guess you're right. I needed to hear you tell me I'm doing the right thing."

"Good. So, come over later, have some coffee and tell me all about your evening. I want to know every tiny detail. I have to go now and get the clothes out of the dryer before they wrinkle. I keep hoping someone will invent paper clothing so Hal and the kids will stop generating so much laundry."

Hope hung up the phone, crossed to the dresser, opened a drawer and tucked the wedding picture beneath her lingerie. If she wanted to make new memories, she had to stash old ones. She took a deep breath, closed the drawer, and headed for her desk and the pile of work. Jerrod's sexy smile lingered in her mind until a whimper from Chloe interrupted. 'You poor thing, is mommy neglecting you?"

****

Amidst steaming pots, a half-chopped salad, and transferring condiments from the refrigerator to the counter, Hope scurried around the kitchen. She'd been seeing Jerrod for over two weeks, when his busy schedule permitted, and for the first time, he was coming for dinner. So far, kisses had been the extent of their passion, but tonight, she had a great after dinner treat planned...and not dessert per se.

She stopped and massaged her brow, forcing her thoughts back to dinner. Did he like chicken? Was he a vegetarian? "Of course, he's not," she mumbled to Chloe, who patiently waited for anything tasty to fall on the floor. "He ordered steak when we went out to eat." But, did he like steamed cauliflower with cheese sauce? So much she still didn't know about him.

Despite her frayed nerves, she organized her meal. She carried the good china to the dining room table where candles already flickered and reflected in the silverware resting on linen napkins. She'd purchased an expensive bottle of red wine the clerk assured her went well with fowl or beef. The man had definitely pooh-poohed her belief about red wine with red meat and white wine with white. If you couldn't trust someone who worked with liquor, who could you trust?

She set the plates in place, centered the silver

candelabra, and then stood back to admire the ambiance.

She snapped her fingers. "Oh, crap, the chicken."

If she didn't get back to the kitchen and check on the breasts, they'd be having blackened meat, and she wasn't sure what wine went with that.

Luckily, the baking meat looked perfectly brown. She lowered the temperature to keep the chicken breasts warm and removed the salad from the fridge. With the burner beneath the corn on simmer, and bread ready to pop into the oven at the last minute, she was as ready as she'd ever be. Would he approve of her choices or hate them?

She took a minute and popped into the bathroom for one last check of her appearance. After losing seven pounds, her jeans fit a lot better, and her v-neck top showed just enough cleavage and was fancy enough for candelabra and wine. Her hair, still perfectly styled, showed just a trace of dampness around her forehead from the kitchen's heat. She dabbed another drop of perfume between her breasts and behind each ear. She smiled as Sandy's comments invaded her mind. Hope's reflection didn't lie. She smiled, liking the shapely, even sexy woman in the mirror. Not bad for someone approaching Denny's Senior Citizen's discount. The doorbell rang. Her breath halted until Chloe's barking earned a scolding. After shooing her into the bedroom and closing the door, Hope drew in a breath and hurried downstairs.

She opened the front door, a *hello* on her lips, but Jerrod swept her into an embrace that launched a passel of butterflies in her stomach. His mouth silenced her greeting with a kiss far too passionate for a couple standing in an open doorway. An image of Sandy in her kitchen window with a pair of binoculars trained on them swept through Hope's mind and she pulled away. "Come in, sweetie. Let's not give the neighbors a show. I'd prefer we make our debut in private." She took hold of his hand, pulled him inside and nudged the door closed with her foot.

"Sorry." He screwed his mouth into an obviously fake frown. "I couldn't wait to hold you again. You've become an addiction, you know?"

"I have?" Flashing a coy smile, she wrapped her arms around his neck. "I've become quite fond of you, too." She lifted her chin and licked her lips. "I'd like another taste of that delightful appetizer, if you don't mind."

Jerrod smiled and leaned down, capturing her lips in his. Slow and obliging, he pressed his lips against her parted ones and probed the recesses of her mouth. His hips ground against hers with the same urgency his kiss displayed.

Hope pulled away, her breath coming in short huffs. "If you keep that up you'll miss the opportunity to judge my culinary skills." She took a step back, splayed her fingers through her bangs and released a long, slow breath. "All I have to do is toss the bread in the oven for a few minutes and dinner is ready."

He pulled her toward him. "We could enjoy dessert first."

Her heartbeat increased in anticipation. His suggestion totally synced with her plans. As much as she wanted to drag him to the bedroom, she broke from his half embrace. "After I toiled all afternoon? I think dessert will wait until we have time to really savor it." She turned toward the kitchen to hide her grimace. "Will you do the honor of pouring the wine?"

She removed the simmering chicken, popped the rolls into the oven, and then returned to the dining area in time to watch him remove his light jacket. He hung it on the coat tree in the foyer. "I'm not late, am I? Traffic was worse than I expected at his hour."

Her gaze appraised him from head to foot, taking in the snug fit of his faded denims, the hugging way his button-up shirt clung to his chest and upper arms, even the enticing glimpse of chest hair she planned to explore later. She licked her lips, but her reaction had nothing to do with the pleasant smells emanating from the kitchen. "No, you timed your arrival perfectly. Dinner will be ready in a few and I'm starving." She failed to add that food wasn't the reason for her suddenly voracious appetite.

Hope picked up one of the filled wine glasses and gestured to the sofa. "Have a seat while I put dinner on the table."

He accepted the goblet and wrinkled his nose. "I've never been one for grape juice...more a beer kinda guy."

She put her hands on her hips. "Well, tonight you're having wine. I spent a small fortune on a bottle, and the least you can do is pretend to love it."

He chuckled and lifted his glass in toast. "Oh, I'm sure wine will become my favorite drink of all time." He eyed the stereo. "Mind if I find some dinner music?"

"Not at all. Something soft and relaxing would be great." She spun and returned to the kitchen.

She filled the salad bowls with trembling hands. A handsome man sat on her couch, waiting for a dinner she planned. She hadn't cooked a meal in a long time, but it wasn't the food that niggled her. What about afterwards? She knew what she wanted, but how did one move from the dining room to the bedroom and not appear obvious? Maybe a little TV or a board game? She shook her head and made a face. Boring came to mind. Oh, if only she knew more about him and what he thought of her. Would taking the next step send him screaming away? One way to find out...let things take their course.

The sexy strains of Kenny G drifted from the

living room. She drifted back into the dining room, carrying the salads, put them in place, and downed a half-glass of wine as liquid courage while Jerrod wasn't looking. She wiped the dampness from her top lip with her fingertips before fetching the hot rolls.

"Dinner is served." The wine's fruity taste lingered in her mouth, warmed her, and made her wonder if maybe she should have purchased a second bottle.

The crisp salad, the bread…nothing on the menu appealed to her. Instead, she watched who she hungered for take a seat opposite her, snap his napkin open and across his lap, and then flash her a smile that melted her heart. Forcing herself, she put her own napkin in place and lifted the bread basket. "Roll?"

****

Hope snuggled up to Jerrod on the sofa. Soft jazz played in the background, and their half-empty wine glasses sat on the coffee table next to his propped feet. Dirty dishes, empty bottle, and wrinkled napkins littered the dining table behind them.

Jerrod lowered his arm from the back of the couch and cupped her shoulder. "Dinner was delicious." He lifted her chin and caught her gaze. "Hmm, beautiful…and she cooks, too. What more could a man ask for?" His breath smelled of sweet merlot.

"Yes, I'm a woman of many talents." She stifled a yawn. The wine made her drowsy and tugged at her eyelids. "However, I've never been able to hold my liquor very well. This wine is like a sleeping-pill." She kept her eyes trained on his face, but slid down and rested her cheek on his chest.

He nodded. "I always suggest a glass of wine before bedtime for patients who have trouble sleeping. Guess that's why I've never cared for it and prefer beer."

His heart beat slowly and evenly against her ear. Who would have guessed that a mere appointment would lead to a cozy night with a handsome doctor? Life was good. She sat up to speak, but noticed he'd reclined his head against the sofa's back and closed his eyes. The sensual beat of the music overcame the wine and heightened her senses. Ever so gently, she slid her fingertips to his shirt buttons. One-by-one, she unfastened them, revealing the tanned and sparsely matted chest she longed to explore.

Jerrod lifted his head and titled his gaze. "Lose something?"

Her cheeks warmed at her brazen behavior. "I...I don't know what came over me." She kneaded his rock-hard abs, sending a quiver through her own stomach.

"Well, I approve of whatever prompted you to

undress me. I like it." He plopped his feet to the floor, swiveled, and drew her into his arms. "May I return the favor?"

Things looked fuzzy through the wine haze. The thick feeling of her tongue suggested she should have eaten more and drank less, but as the clerk at the liquor store, promised, the rich merlot tasted delicious and went down easily. She peered at Jerrod and giggled. "You know, the color of the meat didn't matter."

He arched a well-formed brow. "Huh?"

"The wine…the meat." Her attempt to explain made no sense. She grabbed and waggled her crystal goblet in front of him. "Red wine, white meat…oh, it's not important. We're important." She slurred her words.

"At last something I understand. Yes, we are important." The sincere look in his eyes tugged at her heart.

She set her glass down and laced her fingers behind his neck. "Kiss me."

Instead, Jerrod stood and swept her up into his arms. "I have a better idea." He headed for the bedroom.

Even in her tipsy state, her conscience urged her to say 'no' before things progressed too far—before she surrendered to her growing desires and overwhelming passion. Over three years had passed without a man fulfilling her sexual needs and she turned mute. She wanted him—wanted him to touch her, taste her, make love to her all night. Burying her face against his collar, she breathed his scent and enjoyed the tingle of anticipation between her legs. "Mmm." Her sigh of contentment muffled against his neck.

Jerrod plopped her onto the bed, jolting her out of her amorous thoughts. Her head swam and his image blurred for a moment. She propped herself on an elbow and rested her chin in her palm. "That was quite an unceremonious landing. You trying to tell me something?"

He whipped off his shirt and kicked off his shoes. "Sorry, I guess I'm feeling a little anxious. I forgot I carried precious cargo."

She swallowed hard as he unfastened and removed his pants. His black boxer briefs hugged his muscular thighs. Her gaze traveled the length of him. One didn't get that body sitting behind a desk or rolling around on an examination stool all day. "Do you work out?"

"Occasionally, but I'm dying to show you my favorite type of exercise." He grinned, crawled onto the bed, and stretched out alongside her. His fingers worked at the button on her pants, then the zipper, and within moments, cool air caressed her naked body. Maybe the alcohol dimmed her senses, or the air of comfort with Jerrod kept modesty at bay, but her only thought was how much she wanted him—like a suffocating person craving air.

He hovered over her, propped on his arms, and gazed into her eyes. "You've had a lot of wine, and I respect you too much to take advantage of you. Are you sure about this?"

"Y-yes. I'm not as inebriated as you think. I know quite well who is in my bed, and I also know what I want." Her voice faltered but not her desire. "Make love to me, Jerrod."

His lips met hers but then trailed along her neck, stopping to lave kisses in the hollow of her throat. She hunched against a shiver and sensed goose bumps rising on her arms. She craned her head to the side, inviting him to continue the journey his mouth started. "Oh, that feels so good." What she meant as a thought drifted into the silence and surprised her.

He paused for a moment. "Tastes good, too." Licking his lips, his eyes focused on her breast and his lips locked on a pebbled nipple, swirling his tongue around the tip in a frenzy.

She moaned and arched. Rolling to one side, she silently begged him to pay equal homage to her other breast. With little effort, she snaked her left leg around his firm buttocks and drew him closer.

"Ah, so you like that." His whisper cooled her skin as he switched his lips to the other breast.

"Oh yes, I like it a lot."

Drat her medical knowledge. Terms from transcription and experience mentally described her feelings. Her *clitoris* tingled with desire, her *vagina* grew moist and ready, her *areolas* hardened and puckered. Yes, the terms were all true, but her feelings weren't just about body parts and reactions. Her emotions dealt with attraction, lust, want, need, and God help her, love. She bit her lip to keep the words from spilling out and perhaps spoiling the moment.

Jerrod trailed his lips down her abdomen, past her navel, to the juncture of her thighs. He ducked his head between her legs and lapped at her woman's core. Every nerve in her body cried for sexual release, but not this way. She wanted to feel him inside her—let him explode along with her.

She wriggled from beneath him and took charge, urging him onto his back and rode him until he could perform no more. Amidst heavy breathing and pounding hearts, she rested against his chest until sleep claimed her.

****

Hope woke with a sigh to Jerrod peppering butterfly kisses alongside her neck. "Wake up, sleepyhead. I have to get to the office."

"Oh, is it morning already?" She fluttered her

eyes open and squinted against the brightness.

He was already up and dressed. "Yes it's morning, but I didn't want to leave without thanking you for a wonderful night. You're an amazing woman."

He bent to kiss her but she turned away and pulled the sheet over her mouth. "I refuse to have you leave here, thinking about me having morning breath." She threw back the covers and scampered to the bathroom. The fact she was nude didn't matter. "Give me just a minute," she called over her shoulder.

Returning with fresh breath and brushed hair tucked behind her ears, she molded her body to his. "Okay, now you can kiss me." She lifted her chin.

Moving in close, he cupped her bare behind in warm palms. Her heart hammered in sync with the beat of his against her chest. If only he hadn't dressed yet. Her thoughts traveled back to the pleasure they'd earlier shared.

Jerrod took a step back. "If I don't stop, I'm going to have to take you back to bed."

She pressed her lips together and rubbed them back and forth over one another. "Hmm, I might be convinced to let you."

"Damn work. How about tonight?"

"I'll be here."

"Great. I'll bring takeout." He gave her a quick peck and disappeared through the bedroom door. Chloe looked up from the bed with a cocked head and wagging tail.

"Don't look at me like that, young lady. I didn't do anything I didn't want to."

Outside, his car started. The room still smelled of him...of them. Although his leaving left an emptiness in the pit of her stomach...he'd be back. Hope smiled and slipped into a robe, then turned her attention to changing the satin sheets. With the bedroom refreshed, she headed for the laundry room. "C'mon, Chloe, Momma'll feed you."

Chloe ate with vigor while Hope dealt with the washer. She couldn't wipe away the smile her pleasant memories stirred. The phone rang, and she rushed to the kitchen to answer. She grimaced at the mess from last night's dinner, but only until she eyed the *caller ID*. "Hello, Sandy."

"I thought he'd never leave." Her friend's chuckle drifted through the receiver.

"Don't you have anything better to do than watch my house? I haven't even had my coffee yet."

"Then come over and have a cup with me. Hal just left for work and the boys are at their grandmother's this week. I need details."

"Okay, but first I have to shower and get dressed. I'll need the biggest cup of java you have and a couple aspirins. I have a headache you wouldn't believe."

****

Hope sat in Sandy's kitchen, clutching a steaming mug of coffee with one hand and rubbing her throbbing temple with the other. "I swear I'm never drinking wine again."

"Why? Because alcohol softens your resolve or gives you a hangover?" Sandy bit her lip in a sad attempt to stifle a grin.

"Both." Hope glared at her.

"Seriously, you should ask your doctor about nitrates. Some people can't handle them, and you might be one."

"I'll do that...tonight." Hope took a sip and cringed at the bitter taste.

"He's coming back?"

"Did you think I'd be just a one-night stand? Yes, he's coming back, and I'm shocked you haven't bugged me for more details about last night. Say, where's my aspirin?"

Sandy went to the cabinet and withdrew a bottle. She thrust the pain-reliever at Hope. "Since you brought up the subject, did you—"

"Yes, we did." Hope lowered her gaze and laughed.

"So, I'm nosy. Sue me." She snatched back the bottle when Hope couldn't open the lid. "Line up the arrows and *ta dah*." Sandy shook out two pills, handed them over and sat. "Tell me about last night and don't leave out a single thing."

Hope sighed. "I swear you demand more answers than my mother did when I had my first date."

****

Hope tilted the headphones onto her neck and leaned back in her well-used desk chair. Her back ached from hours of sitting at the computer and she, in general, felt like crap. Thoughts of Jerrod had become a major distraction, and the time they spent together had put her behind schedule. No one had complained yet, and she planned to make sure none of her clients did. Jerrod couldn't very well bitch, since he was part of the problem, but transcription was her livelihood and she'd somehow lost sight of that.

Keeping busy all morning hadn't helped the nauseous feeling pass. Instead, she felt worse than before. At least, all the chart notes were typed up, but delivery would have to wait until tomorrow when she felt better. The clock showed it was only five-thirty p.m., but her bed beckoned.

Chloe slept next to her feet, so she tried not to move them, but her churning stomach didn't have the same regard for the pup. Someone knocked on the door. Hope cringed. She certainly didn't feel like entertaining company. Standing, she covered her mouth while bile rose in her throat. Chloe, now wide awake, yipped at the continued rapping. Swallowing hard, Hope crossed to the door and peered through the peephole. "Oh, Sandy, not now," she grumbled.

There was no use pretending not to be home. Hope's car was in the driveway and Sandy knew her every move. Hope opened the door. "Hi, enter at risk of getting sick. I think I have the flu."

"You look like hell." Sandy took a step back and bent to pet Chloe.

"Thanks, I need that." Hope hugged herself against a chill. "I feel all achy, tired, and sick to my stomach. I must have picked up a bug somewhere."

"Or, one rode in on a doctor's coat." Sandy chuckled.

"Very funny. Did you want something or did you just come to make jokes?"

"I need to borrow a cup of sugar. I'm making cookies for the boys and ran out."

"Wait here. I'll get some for you...or you can come in if you dare." Hope turned and headed for the kitchen.

The door closed. "From the look of your desk, you've been a busy girl." Sandy's voice indicated she'd decided to risk the germs.

Hope returned with a cup of sugar. "Yes, and I'm all caught up now. I'm not taking on any more clients. I can barely keep up with the ones I have."

"Especially now that you have a new love interest." Sandy waggled an eyebrow. "Are you transcribing for him, too?"

Hope shook her head. "No, we decided it wasn't a good idea to engage in a business relationship as well as a personal one." The bile rose in her throat again and she gulped it down.

She was about to give her friend the bum's rush, but Sandy took the cup of sugar and opened the front door. "Gotta run. I have a batch in the oven and don't want them to burn. You'd better take a couple aspirin and get some rest. Call me if you need anything."

Hope blew Sandy a kiss and closed the door. Jerrod was at a medical convention all week, and although she missed him, now was a good time to be sick...if there ever was a good time. How ironic. When she needed a doctor, he wasn't around. Her stomach churned, and she ran for the bathroom.

After losing her lunch, Hope turned back the covers on her bed and crawled beneath them. The phone rang just as she'd managed to doze off.

"Hi, sweet thing." Jerrod's deep voice increased her chills. "I had a break between sessions and called to tell you how much I miss you."

"Hmmm, miss you too." She responded in a voice as weak as she felt.

"Are you okay?"

"Flu, I think. I've felt ill all day. Tired, achy, chills, out of sorts."

"Have you taken your temperature?"

"No." She raised her hand to her forehead. "I don't feel hot."

"How about if you measure your temp with a thermometer instead of by touch?"

"Okay, I will when I hang up. When are you coming home?"

"On Saturday, but promise me if you don't feel better tomorrow, you'll call the office and see Dr. Halliday. He's on call for me while I'm gone."

"Isn't he an OB-GYN like you?"

"Yes, but he also has a family practice specialty."

"Okay, I promise I'll call, but I'm sure this is only a bug and I'll feel better tomorrow."

"I'll let you go so you can get some rest. Drink plenty of fluids and check that temperature. I want you to be well when I get back." A sexy chuckle followed.

"Is that all I am to you, a booty call?"

"You know better than that." His tone turned serious

"I was only kidding, but you realize we've never really discussed our feelings outside the bedroom." She immediately wanted to bite her tongue for pressing the point.

"We'll just have to do that, won't we? Honestly,

Hope, I miss you like crazy and can't wait to get back so I can see you."

"Me too. Hurry up."

She hung up before the words she wanted to say slipped out. Telling him she loved him seemed natural, but maybe he didn't share the same feelings. Like lust? Certainly, but love? He'd never even hinted as much.

Her stomach lurched again. She curled into a ball and closed her eyes. If she slept maybe she'd feel better. Unfortunately her insides had other plans. She barely made it to the bathroom before she heaved again. Kneeling before the *porcelain throne*, she rested her cheek on her hand and stared into the toilet bowl. She hadn't been this ill in a long time, and throwing up sucked. When the nausea subsided, she crept back to bed and sank into welcome oblivion with Chloe curled next to her.

****

Hope awoke to the usual Friday clatter of trashcans being emptied. She knuckled her eyes and yawned. Why garbage trucks came at seven a.m. remained a mystery.

Her mouth tasted pasty and dry, and her empty stomach grumbled. She swiveled around, dropped her feet to the floor, and stood. The room spun, and she sagged back onto the bed and held her head. "What's wrong with me, Chloe" she groaned. The pup licked her paw and ignored her mistress.

Hope needed something to settle her stomach but had nothing in the house but milk, tea, and coffee. Maybe Sandy had something better. She'd be up, getting the kids off to school. Hope reached for the phone and dialed.

"It's me, Sandy. Do you have any soda in the house? Preferably something with bubbles."

"Still not feeling well, eh?"

"I was hoping for a twenty-four hour bug. No such luck. I'm so dizzy, I can hardly stand."

"How about some Seven-Up?"

"That would be great. Just ring and leave it by the front door."

"Oh, get real. You already exposed me yesterday when I came for sugar. I'll be right over. I'll bring some soup, too. What are friends for if not take care of you when you're sick?"

"You're a doll. I hope I don't have to return the favor."

"No worries. My immune system has been through everything with the kids. I'm on my way."

Within minutes, the doorbell sounded. Hope clung to the door as she let Sandy in, then padded right back to bed. Ice cubes tinkling and cupboard doors slamming clued Hope to her friend's whereabouts.

Sandy appeared carrying a tray. "You really need to eat something. I decided chicken broth might be easier on your stomach than something more bulky." She set the tray on Hope's lap. "Hope you don't mind the diet soda. It's all I buy."

The soup's aroma wafted upward with the steam and made her stomach churn. Hope wrinkled her nose and turned her face. "Oh, I can't eat. Take it away. Just leave the soda." She lifted the glass from the tray and took a sip.

Sandy swept the tray up and out of the room, and then returned. "Have you taken your temperature?"

"You sound just like Jerrod. I'm not hot. Feel me."

Sandy pressed her fingers against Hope's brow. "You're right." She stepped back. "Can I get you anything else before I go? I have to get the kids to school."

"No, I'll be fine." She took another sip. "I think the soda is helping settle my stomach."

"Good, I'll check back on you later and bring more pop and maybe some crackers."

"Thanks, pal. You're the best."

****

Still clad in her bathrobe, Hope answered the

door. She expected Sandy but instead, Jerrod stood on her doorstep with a big smile and a bouquet of yellow roses. "Are you still sick, sweetie?"

Why hadn't he called? She fluffed her tousled hair and tightened her sash, certain she looked as green as the wrapper she wore. "I fear my appearance speaks for itself. Are you sure you want to come in?"

"I'm a doctor, remember? I deal with sick people all the time." He closed the door behind him and put an arm around her waist. "Let's get you back to bed." He laid the roses on the entry table.

She flashed a weak smile. "Any other time, you getting me to bed might sound inviting, bu…."

"I prefer we reserve that kind of thinking for a time when you're up for it." He laughed and tightened his grasp. Chloe growled and retreated under the coffee table.

In the bedroom, Jerrod flipped back the bed covers. "Make yourself comfortable. I'm going to go put your flowers in water. Be right back."

Hope dropped the robe on the floor and sank back into bed. She plumped the pillow, leaned back, heaved a sigh, and then pulled the blanket over her legs.

Jerrod returned with the long-stemmed yellow beauties in a crystal vase and set them on the dresser. "Maybe these will help cheer you."

"They're beautiful. Thank you."

"My pleasure." He perched on the bed's edge.

Despite an attempt at smiling, her spirits dipped. Yellow roses instead of red? Did he know what difference flower colors meant?

He patted her hand. "Tell the doctor all about your symptoms. I'm pretty sure you have that flu that's making the rounds, but why pass up a free exam?"

She forced a grin. "This all started with chills, weakness, achy muscles, and worked into nausea. Everything but this sickly knot in my stomach has pretty much improved...except I feel like I don't have the strength to lift a pebble." She rubbed her midsection.

"How long since you've eaten?"

"I can't eat. Nothing stays down." She grimaced.

"Are you drinking lots of fluids? You don't want to get dehydrated."

"Yes, *doctor.* I've downed enough Seven-Up to float a boat."

"Good." He patted her leg. "If you don't improve in a day or so, I want you to come in for blood tests."

She bolted upright and stared at him. "Why? Do you think there's something seriously wrong with me?"

Jerrod pressed a hand against her shoulder and eased her back down. "If I thought that, I'd haul your charming derriere in right this minute."

"Charming, is it?" Her muscles eased and she sank into her feathered backrest.

"I couldn't think of anything else during that boring seminar." He squeezed her hand.

"I thought of you the entire time, too. I'm sorry I'm sick."

"Me too, but I'm sure you'll be better tomorrow. I'm gonna take off so you can rest...or so I don't crawl into bed and take advantage of you." His gaze lingered on her face until he blinked and took a breath. "I must have a ton of paperwork to catch up on at the office, so I'll be there if you need anything." He leaned and grazed her cheek with a kiss

She pulled her lips into an exaggerated pout. "Okay, but when I get better you owe me a much better smooch than that."

"Deal." He rose, winked a sexy eye and waved. "I'll lock the door behind me."

"You'd better or Sandy will be over here grilling me for information."

"Huh?"

"Never mind. It's not important. Sandy's my neighbor."

****

Hope woke on Monday morning feeling much

better, although still a little queasy. Jerrod had called several times over the weekend to check on her, but had stayed busy at his office. She rose and swigged the remaining soda from the glass on her nightstand and, her jaw set, headed for the shower. Afterwards, she'd still have time to do some transcribing before meeting Jerrod for lunch. She'd gotten several new tapes in the mail and was behind again.

After stepping into the stall, she closed the door and let the water's heat sink into her pores. Thoughts of Jerrod and getting back into their routine warmed her blood. God, help her, she'd fallen in love with him, and if the look in his eyes meant anything, he had feelings for her, too. At least she prayed so.

****

Hope sat in the diner, amidst the tinkling of silverware, chorused voices and waitresses scurrying around, and waited for Jerrod. He'd reserved a table for them, and now she waited to see his handsome face in the doorway. Her morning passed quickly, being engrossed in transcribing, and she'd barely given any thought to how she felt. Now the mixed aromas from plates being served around her made her stomach roil. She choked back bitter bile and surveyed the room for a restroom sign.

Jerrod waved and approached the table. "Hi."

He bent and kissed her cheek and then pulled out the chair across from her and sat. His gaze swept her face. "You look...pale, but better. How are you feeling?"

"Fine." She lied. "Let's not talk about me. How about you? Did you get caught up with your paperwork?"

He held up a finger and rubbed a noticeable indentation. "See this? It's from signing prescriptions. I spent the entire weekend at my desk, but I can finally see the top of it again."

"Poor baby," she cooed.

He reached across and grasped her hands. "You have no idea how I've missed spending time with you. You've become very special to me."

A pang of sorry plucked at her, wanting to mean more than that to him. Pets were *special*, a favorite sweater was *special*. Hell, even the restaurant had a *special* of the day posted on the blackboard near the hostesses' desk. She gulped back tears and smiled. "I feel the same."

The waitress stood tableside, her pen poised for their orders. Jerrod gestured for Hope to go first. The thought of food sickened her, and she slid the menu aside. "I'll have a club soda, please."

Jerrod's brow rose. "Is that all?"

"I'm really not hungry, but please, you go ahead and eat."

He shrugged and looked to the waitress. "I'll

have a hamburger medium well, and a glass of water with lemon."

The woman walked away with the menus tucked under her arm, and Jerrod turned a pensive glare on Hope. "Are you sure you're okay?

"I'm fine, really. I shouldn't have eaten so much breakfast." Where was the harm in a little white lie? She hadn't had anything in days other than Seven-Up. Maybe later, she'd try and eat something, but not now.

Forgetting her upset stomach, Hope chattered while Jerrod ate. She so enjoyed his company and the envying stares from other women, and he seemed to enjoy hearing about Sandy and the relationship she and Hope had formed over the years.

"Maybe you could have your friend check in on you for me this evening. I have to stop by the hospital and check in on a few patients."

As much as she cherished their time together, relief flooded through her at his announcement. Throwing up within hearing distance of him didn't appeal to her. She tried to look disappointed. "Oh, I was so hoping we could cuddle up and watch a movie or something, but..."

"Well, you know things like this come with the profession. I'm sure you understand."

"Of course, but I'll miss you."

He pulled a twenty from his wallet, threw it on the table, stood, and walked around and pulled out her chair. Together, they walked to her car, where he kissed her and promised to call.

Hope drove straight home, changed into her pajamas, and phoned her neighbor. "Sandy, I'm getting scared. I can't seem to shake whatever this is that I have."

"Oh, Hope. Don't fret. You probably still have that virus that's going around. I hear it takes time to get over it. Did you tell Jerrod how you're feeling?"

"No, he doesn't know I'm still not feeling well. We had lunch together today and he commented on my lack of color, but...."

"Why are you so freaked out?"

Hope sighed into the phone. "I transcribed notes this morning on someone who has stomach cancer. My symptoms are too similar to ignore."

"Oh, God, Hope. Don't tell me after all these months on the job you're going to become a hypochondriac and identify with every symptom you type."

"Of course not. I've had the flu before and never felt like this. Just the thought of food sickens me."

Sandy snickered. "Sounds like a great way to lose weight."

"Don't kid around. I'm serious."

"Sorry, I'm just trying to lighten the moment. I have no idea what to tell you. If you hadn't said you're going through menopause, I might think you're pregnant. I nearly heaved myself to death with both boys."

"There's no way. I haven't had periods in months." She paused for a moment.

"Are you still there?"

"Hmm, yes, I'm here. I wonder if I'm having a reaction to the blood pressure medicine Jerrod prescribed. But wouldn't he have mentioned that as a possibility?"

"Not if you didn't tell him you're still sick. He's a doctor, not a mind reader. Call him and ask."

"I will...I will."

Hope hung up, intent on calling a doctor, but not Jerrod. If she suffered from some dire ailment, she couldn't bear having him be the one to tell her. She went to her desk and dialed the number of one of the general practitioners for whom she transcribed. His receptionist answered promptly.

"Hi, this is Hope Harrison. I do transcriptions for Dr. McMahon. I wonder if he might have an open appointment this afternoon. I need to drop off some tapes and if he could see me at the same time, that would be great."

"Sure, Hope. It's me, Misty, the person who normally gives you the tapes. We'll fit you in. What seems to be the problem?"

"I wish I knew. I've been ill for over a week and

don't seem to be getting any better."

"I'll note the appointment schedule and we'll see you at three thirty if that works."

"That's perfect. I'll see you then."

Hope hung up, and turned on her computer. With her headphones in place, she typed with determination. Worry stole her focus and made her more aware of how she felt. She finally grabbed a novel and climbed back into bed. She turned pages until two-thirty, but couldn't remember what she'd read. She changed clothes, brushed her hair, grabbed her purse and the doctor's tapes and left for her appointment. She nibbled her bottom lip all the way there. What if she did have cancer?

There weren't many people in the waiting area. Hope had barely finished her paperwork when Misty called her back into the exam room. She handed her forms to the brown-eyed girl wearing colorful scrubs and her blonde hair in a ponytail, and envied Misty's youth. "Maybe I'm just getting old."

Misty giggled. "Oh, I'm sure that's not it. Doctor McMahon will be right with you."

Hope stepped up and sat on the paper-covered table. The doctor appeared within only a few minutes, carrying a folder. She smiled at the chubby, gray-haired man who always exuded a good mood.

"Well, Hope, I expected to see you this week, but not as a patient. Didn't you tell me you have a family doctor?"

"Yes, I did...do have one. I...I want to discuss my current situation with someone else."

"I'm happy you thought of me. So, what seems to be troubling you?" He sat on a rolling stool and gave her a pensive look.

She massaged her brow and moistened her dry lips. "I've been sick for nearly two weeks. Can't stop vomiting, feel weak, dizzy, and I'm just not myself. I'm really worried what I have could be serious."

The doctor removed a pen from his lab coat pocket and jotted notes in her chart. He glanced up. "You know, there are several viruses going around right now."

"I realize that, and at first I thought I'd caught one, but I'm a trained nurse and something screams this isn't the flu."

He nodded. "Well, we can't ignore those screams, can we? Let's do some blood work and see what's going on. I'll put a rush on your test and we should have the results back tomorrow. First though, let me listen to your heart and lungs."

She took breaths in and out as he requested.

"Okay, now lay back for me."

Hope reclined against the raised back of the exam table, crinkling the paper with her movement while the doctor palpated and listened to her stomach. She fought rising bile when he pushed on her midsection and grew dizzy when he gave her a hand up. Her worry increased as he jotted down more notes, his forehead furrowed. Oh, how she wished for the comfort of her bed and Jerrod's embrace.

Dr. McMahon turned to her. "Your heart and lungs sound fine. I hear a lot of gurgling in your belly, but that could just be the digestive process. Have you eaten today?"

"No." She shook her head and lowered her gaze. "But, I feel like I have."

He touched her shoulder. "I'm sure what ails you is nothing to worry about. Some of these bugs hold on a while longer than others, and the blood test will tell us if that's the case. I can give you something for nausea if you'd like."

"Please." She clasped her hands beneath her chin. "I can barely function when I feel like I'm going to upchuck any minute."

He wrote out the script and handed it to her. "Take one pill twice a day. I'll have the nurse come and draw your blood. Someone will call you tomorrow with the results. Feel better soon." He patted her hand on the way out the door.

****

Hope woke with a queasy stomach, but not nearly as bad as before taking the medicine Dr.

McMahon prescribed. Transcribing, she sat, lost in thought at her computer. The phone rang and Hope nearly jumped out of her chair. "Hello." She clutched her chest.

"This is Misty from Dr. McMahon's office. I have your test results, and—"

"Is there something wrong?" Hope didn't give her time to finish.

"Quite the contrary. Congratulations, you're going to be a mother."

She gasped, speechless for a moment. "B...but, that c...can't possibly be... I–"

"Tests don't lie." Misty chuckled. Dr. Mac wants you to schedule a follow-up with your family doctor, and in the meantime, he'd like you to get started on prenatal vitamins. He's concerned you're bordering on anemia. He's called a prescription into the drug store you listed."

""O...okay, Misty."

"Do you have any questions?"

A million whirred through Hope's mind, but she had answers for most of them. "No, but if I think of any, I'll call back." She clicked the disconnect button and put the cordless phone back in its charger. With her elbows on the desktop, she leaned into her palms and stared into space. Could she really be...pregnant? She had no words. What...how...could this be? Hope closed her eyes.

Pregnant? No way. She was too old to be a mother. Her heart hammered. "Tests don't lie," she told Chloe in the same tone Misty used. She was right, especially when symptoms backed up the results. Hope stood and paced. What on earth was she going to do?

Sandy! Hope needed someone to talk to or explode. She grabbed the phone and dialed her friend's number.

"Hi, there. I was just thinking about you. Feeling any better?" Sandy sounded her usual, chipper self.

"I need you to come over before I do something insane."

"I'm on my way."

Hope opened the door before Sandy had a chance to knock.

"What's wrong?"

Hope covered her mouth to stifle the scream growing deep inside.

Sandy rushed into the house, her brow furrowed. "You look as though you've seen a ghost. What's wrong?"

Tears welled in Hope's eyes. She swallowed the lump in her throat. I...I'm pregnant." She walked to the sofa and sagged down on an end cushion.

"You're what?" Sandy's eyes widened to the size of silver dollars. She followed and sat next to Hope. "Are you sure? I thought you—"

"Yeah, so did I. I haven't had a period for months, but I just got a call about the results of a blood test. Surprise!" She covered her face. "How could I possibly be pregnant?"

Sandy patted Hope's shoulder. "Well, we both know how *it* happened."

Her attempt at humor fell short. Hope lowered her hands and glared at Sandy. "This isn't funny. What do I do?"

"Does Jerrod know?"

Hope shook her head. "God, no. I can't tell him. He'll think I did this to trap him."

"He's the father. He deserves to know."

"Maybe so, but I can't take that chance."

"Well, I still think you should tell him. He's going to find out eventually, and then what will he think?"

"Oh, Sandy. I'm so confused. I have to think this through more carefully. I don't even know what I'm going to do yet."

"What do you mean?" Sandy straightened, her face sober.

"Women my age have a greater chance of having a child with birth defects. I don't know if I could handle that."

"For God's sake, Hope. When did you get so negative about things? There's just as good a chance you'll have a normal, happy baby. You *must* discuss this with Jerrod before you make such a drastic decision. He deserves to have a say."

Hope rose on shaky legs. "Thanks for coming over, but right now I need some time alone to digest all this. Can I call you later?"

Sandy stood. "I understand, but please, please, call Jerrod. He's part of any decision you make, and remember, I'm here when you need me." She hugged Hope and then left.

****

Hope re-checked the address on the building across the street from where she parked. Only gold numbers marked the red brick. Nestled between a greasy automobile repair shop and a rundown bakery, no one would expect to find a medical clinic.

Her knuckles turned white from gripping the steering wheel. Her decision hadn't come easy, but what she did with her body was her business. Now she questioned her choice.

After Sandy left, Jerrod called and invited Hope to dinner. She'd begged off, saying she was too far behind on her transcription and needed to catch up. It wasn't a total lie, but she spent the rest of the afternoon and evening researching options on the Internet. One sentence embedded itself in her mind. "The risks of bearing a child with certain chromosomal disorders increase with age."

No matter how positive she tried to be, statistics carried more weight than imagining the future. One out of twelve children born to women over the age of forty-nine had Down's Syndrome. One out of seven suffered some other chromosomal defect.

Air whooshed through her pursed lips as she pictured the challenges of raising a mentally retarded child. A younger Hope would never consider terminating a pregnancy, but the older Hope wasn't that strong, and Jerrod deserved better than having to take part in such a difficult decision. This was her mess, and she'd clean it up. She shouldn't have been so careless.

When traffic cleared, she grabbed her purse, exited the car and dashed across the street. She paused with her hand on the clinic's doorknob. Was this really the solution? She took a deep breath and entered.

"Good afternoon. May I help you?" A woman, who appeared to be in her thirties, looked up from a desk behind a glass partition and flashed a welcoming smile.

Hope crossed to the counter, eyeing the myriad of literature displayed there. Her mouth turned to cotton. "I...I'd like some information please."

"Of course. Feel free to peruse any of our printed material, or if you prefer, I can set an appointment for you to meet with one of our counselors."

Hope managed to return the woman's smile. "I think I'd like to look through some of the pamphlets first, if you don't mind."

"Whatever you'd like." The clerk gestured to the colorful brochures. "Help yourself and have a seat. If you have any questions, let me know." She slid her chair over to her computer and returned to her typing.

Hope gathered several tri-folds and glanced around the empty waiting room. She sat in the chair closest to the wall, put her handbag on the floor, and read. The impersonal wording made the process medically clear–almost as if no human being was involved. Time was of the essence—the emphasis on that warning appeared several times in every piece of literature. "The first trimester." Hope's voice sliced the silence and she went back to reading in silence.

The door opened and Hope glanced up. A freckled-face teenager entered with an older woman whose creased brow and narrowed eyes clearly showed her disdain. The two were directed behind a second door, leaving Hope to wonder what happened beyond the waiting area. She went back to perusing the pamphlets, but trembling fingers made it difficult to pull the slick pages apart.

She paused and inhaled, hoping her pulse would slow. Her gaze wandered the walls and the posters plastered there. Happy faces smiled down at her and captions encouraged her to make the right choice. If only she could, but this place gave her the creeps.

She turned her attention back to reading, and cringed at the description of vacuuming a fetus from the womb. The thought appalled her, but so did the fright of bearing a deformed child. God, she needed Jerrod and his wisdom, but she didn't dare call. This was her decision to make.

Her shoulders squared, Hope gathered the literature together, stood and returned to the counter where she replaced each pamphlet in its respective holder.

The young woman glanced up from her computer, peering over glasses she hadn't previously worn. "Do you have any questions, ma'am?"

"No I think I found the answers I need. Thank you for your help." Hope, standing straighter than when she entered, walked out the door, albeit on shaky legs.

Outside, she leaned against the building, pondering her choice. She'd go home and call for an appointment. The burden of choice lifted, but somehow she didn't feel any better. Right or wrong, she knew what had to be done.

Dodging oncoming traffic, she zigzagged to where her car was parked, and then drove home. She made only one stop: the drugstore for vitamins. In her driveway, she waved at Sandy, who smiled through her kitchen window, and then hurried into the house. She found the phone where she'd left it and dialed.

"Misty, this is Hope Harrison again. For reason's I'd rather not discuss, I can't make an appointment with my own OB/GYN. I wonder if you can recommend another doctor for me?"

"Of course, Dr. Gerritt is here in this building. We refer patients to him all the time. He's quite good, and if you'd like, I'll make arrangements for you to see him. Acting on behalf of Dr. McMahon, I'm sure I can get you in sooner than if you called yourself."

"I'd appreciate it. I picked up my vitamins today, but I know how important prenatal care is. I'll wait to hear from you." She hung up and went into the kitchen.

Clutching the vitamin bottle in her hand, Hope bemoaned the next task before her. Jerrod. She had to face him...and lie. She gulped down a pill with water, tucked the remaining supply in a cabinet, and put on the teakettle. The phone rang and she knew it was him. Her hands trembled as she answered.

"Sure, I'd love to see you tonight. I have something important to tell you." Better to get it over with than worry about it. "I'll see you around seven. Have a nice rest of your day."

****

Hope's stomach churned but this time from nerves. The nausea medicine had either cured her previous problem or the morning sickness had passed. She'd practically worn a hole in the carpet, pacing in front of the sofa. She'd imagined a dozen different ways to tell Jerrod what was on her mind, but none sounded right—too scripted or rehearsed. Chloe curled on the couch, watching Hope's every move.

A knock on the door caused Hope's breath to catch. She gazed through the peephole and saw Jerrod's ruggedly handsome face. Her heart ached.

She opened the door and made a sweeping gesture. "Please, come in."

He stepped inside, snaked an arm around her waist and pulled her close. "At last, I get to hold you. I've missed this." The timbre of his voice, as always, made her weak with desire.

He leaned in for a kiss, his eyes sparkling like a mischievous child. Hope closed her eyes, fighting tears, knowing this one might be their last. She struggled against the passion stirring her very soul as his tongue met and mingled with her own.

"He pulled away and studied her face. What's the matter? You look so sad and that wasn't your usual best effort."

"Come and sit. I'll explain." She grasped his

hand and pulled him into the living room. Chloe jumped to the floor and disappeared into the bedroom.

Jerrod plopped down on the sofa and peered up at her beneath long, dark lashes. "I'm not going to like this, am I?

"I...I'm afraid not." She sat next to him but not as close as normal. I...we...ca—" Emotions lumped in her throat and choked off her intended declaration.

"What's wrong, Hope?"

He reached for her hand and she inched back from his touch.

"Tell me, please?"

Taking a deep breath, she followed it with a slow exhalation, fighting for time. She squared her shoulders and met his worried gaze. "We can't see each other anymore."

****

"What?" Jerrod jumped to his feet and glared down at her. "Not see each other anymore? Why on earth not?"

She peered up at him, her heart pounding and tears welling. "I...I think it's best."

"For whom? Telling me you think *it's best* doesn't explain a thing."

The veins in his neck bulged. Her mind spun.

How could she break off their relationship without divulging the real reason? God, she adored him, even if he never said he loved her. Clearly, he felt something strong for her to be this upset. She stared into her lap. "I...I've given my decision a lot of thought and I don't see a future for us. I think it would be easier if we called things off now before either of us gets too attached." The lie clung to her tongue like peanut butter on a spoon. She glanced up to see his reaction.

He paced. "I can't believe this is happening. I'm already attached and I thought you felt the same." He stopped and stared at her. "I love you, Hope. I don't want us to be apart."

She gasped. He'd said the words she dreamed of hearing, but his timing was all wrong. Steeling herself against his blue eyes, his trim frame, his good looks, but most of all, his heartfelt words, she stood and locked gazes with him. "I'm sorry, but I'm not changing my mind. I need you to leave, please."

If he didn't go, her resolve would crumble and she'd beg him to stay, take her to bed and show her how much he loved her. On unsteady legs, she walked to the door and opened it. "Goodbye, Jerrod."

He rushed past her without a word. His shoulders sagged and he sniffed, but he didn't even glance in her direction. She shut the door, leaned against it, and slid down into a tearful heap on the floor. Jerrod was gone and her heart felt as though someone had punched her in the chest. She hugged herself and rocked back and forth. "Oh, Jerrod, I do love you. I do, I do."

****

Hope sat on the couch, her swollen feet propped up on the coffee table. As became habit, she massaged her enlarged belly while glancing over her shoulder into the kitchen. "I don't know what I would've done without you all these months, Sandy. You're the best friend I've ever had."

Sandy carried in two cups of steaming tea on a serving tray and sat beside her friend. "Here you go—one sugar and a little milk, and as for being your best friend, that goes two ways. I'm so excited you asked me to be your daughter's Godmother." She patted Hope's stomach. "I still think you should have given Jerrod the option of staying or going."

Hope lowered her feet to the floor and reached for a teacup. "I know, I know. You've told me constantly these past seven months. You can't think this has been easy on me especially when he kept calling for a whole month after I ended things. I guess he finally gave up and accepted I wasn't going to change my mind, since I haven't heard from him anymore."

Sandy raised her cup and blew a wisp of steam

away. "Jerrod has to be confused over your sudden change of heart." She took a sip and lowered her tea. "He probably thinks he did something wrong. Don't you miss him?"

"Of course I do, but I couldn't risk telling him. He's such a good-hearted person. He would have wanted to marry me, and I couldn't stand wondering if he'd proposed out of love or obligation. Does that make sense?"

"I suppose it does, but you'll still never know, and now you'll be raising this child alone." Sandy clucked her tongue against her teeth. "Good thing I have lots of mothering experience."

"I knew I'd be on my own when I made the decision. I'm not worried. There isn't a single mother out there who has it better than I do. Because of Alan's insurance policy, I'm in good shape, and I even have the ideal job—working at home. Of course, I have my baby's Godmother to count on." Hope flashed a grin at Sandy.

Sandy drained her cup and then placed it on the tray. "Well, the Godmother needs to get home and check on her own children, and I have to get dinner on before the "Godfather" comes home and finds nothing cooking." She stood, picked up the tray and held it in front of Hope. "Drink up so I can put these cups in the dishwasher. Do you need anything else before I leave?"

Hope placed her cup next to Sandy's, leaned back and rested her feet on the coffee table again. "Nope." She massaged both sides of her stomach and arched her back. "My nameless child and I'll be just fine, thanks. I'm gonna spend a little more time on the computer and then turn in. I get so tired these days."

Sandy laughed. "Just wait another month or so. You don't know tired, yet."

As soon as the door closed behind Sandy, Hope stood and tugged her maternity top over her growing belly. She'd already gained fifteen pounds and appeared further along than seven months. Waddling to the computer, she winced as the baby gave a swift kick to her bladder. She changed direction and headed for the bathroom. Chloe trailed along behind.

Hope was about to sit at her computer when a searing pain stole her breath. She inhaled and steadied herself, then dropped into her chair. "It's only Braxton Hicks," she puffed.

In books she'd read, women often mistook those pains for labor. The contractions were normal and nothing to be alarmed over, but she turned to her keyboard and did a search for the term, looking for further reassurance. After reading about them, she relaxed, put a tape in her machine, donned her headphones and typed with furry to whittle down her workload. After only half a page, another jolt shot though her. She pushed back from the desk and doubled over. "Whew, little one. I prefer your gentle ballet kicks. Take it easy on your old mom."

She moved from her office area to the sofa and stretched out. She'd been on her feet most of the day, shopping for groceries and baby clothes. Anything for wee ones drew her in like a magnet, especially after the ultra-sound that pronounced everything normal and that her baby was a girl. The closet in the nursery overflowed with frilly little dresses and the drawers were stuffed with pink layette pieces. If the child turned out male, he was going to be really humiliated. She chuckled.

Hope sat on the couch for a while and had no more pains. Her stomach rumbled, since hours had passed since she ate lunch. She pulled herself up and tottered into the kitchen, made a bowl of cereal. Quick and easy, dining on packaged foods allowed more time to work. She returned to her computer, typed until her back couldn't stand sitting another minute, and then she went to bed.

****

Hope moaned and came awake. She rolled onto her back and grimaced at the painful stab in her lower abdomen. Had someone tied a rope around her stomach and tied it to the bumper of a departing car? The pain felt like it. She massaged her belly, noting the skin was tight as a drum. Turning to her side, she hoped the discomfort would pass, but another contraction jolted her. This one took her breath away. Something sticky and wet oozed between her legs. She reached to the nightstand and turned on the lamp. Pulling herself into a sitting position, she threw back the covers and gasped. A red stain darkened the sheet beneath her. "Oh, my God, this isn't right."

Chloe sat up, cocked her head, and proceeded over and sniffed at the scarlet spot until Hope shooed her away. She eased off the bed and went into the bathroom. After washing herself, she donned another gown and then waddled back to the nightstand and dialed Sandy.

"Hullo." Her friend answered in a voice slurred from sleep.

"It's me. I need your help."

"What time is it?"

"Three a.m., but I wouldn't call if I didn't need you."

"What's wrong?" The grogginess in Sandy's voice disappeared.

"I'm having pains and bleeding. What should I do?"

"You're the nurse, don't you know?"

"Maternity wasn't my forte, and if I knew, would I be calling you? Can you please take me to the hospital?"

"I'll throw on some clothes and be right there."

****

Hope's feet strained against the floorboard with each wave of pain. Sandy cast a sidelong glance at her, oncoming traffic shining in her eyes. "Hold on, we're almost there."

The contraction ceased. Hope took a deep breath. "This isn't supposed to be happening for another two months." Tears spilled from her blurry eyes. "What if something is terribly wrong and I lose the baby?"

Sandy stretched her hand over and patted Hope's. "You aren't going to lose my Goddaughter. The doctors will know what to do. Be brave and have faith."

Hope clenched her teeth as another pain gripped her. A sigh of relief whooshed out when Sandy drove into the hospital driveway and stopped in front of the emergency room door. She'd called ahead, and attendants waited with a wheelchair. They whisked Hope out of the car and wheeled her inside. Hope held tight to Sandy's words about not losing faith although inside, Hope quivered like her grandma's grape jelly.

A nurse helped Hope onto a Gurney and covered her with a blanket straight from the warmer. The soothing heat stopped her nervous shaking. The woman in scrubs wrapped a blood pressure cuff around Hope's left arm, and then reached beneath the covers and attached monitors to her bared stomach. The sound of a fast and steady beep filled the room. The baby's constant heartbeat proved a welcome sound and gave Hope strength. The tightening of the band around her arm added an additional chirp to the mix, but her gaze fixated on the baby's monitor instead of the measure of her blood pressure.

"How far along are you?" The nurse asked.

"Only seven months. "Hope turned a pleading gaze on her. "Please tell me my baby is okay."

The nurse patted her hand. "Who's your doctor?"

"Dr. John Gerritt."

"I'll go see if I can contact him, but first I need to get an IV started."

Hope stifled a groan when the nurse inserted the needle into her vein. The task was something Hope had done many times during her career, but this was the first time she'd been on the receiving end of the stick.

Another woman appeared with a syringe and injected the contents into Hope's IV tube. Within minutes, she became groggy and relaxed. Either her contraction had abated or the medicine numbed the pain.

"Okay, Ms. Harrison, I'm going to step out and

call your doctor, but in case Dr. Gerritt can't get here in time, we do have an obstetric doc on duty. Don't worry, either way, you'll be in capable hands."

"Where's m…my…my friend." Hope's tongue was thick and her mind hazy.

"In the waiting room. Would you like me to get her?"

"Please." Hope's head lolled to the side. The room looked slanted.

"Hope?" Sandy stood next to the Gurney and peered down at her. "How do you feel?"

"Tired. Whatever they gave me is great stuff. You should try it."

Sandy laughed. "I think I'll pass. One of us has to be in control of our faculties." She cupped Hope's chin and turned her head. "They're going to admit you. I filled out the papers for you and gave them the insurance card from your purse."

"T…thank you."

"And Hope…I caught a glimpse of the OB doctor as I came in here. It's…it's Jerrod."

****

Hope's eyes fluttered in an attempt to open them. Had she heard right? "Wh…what?"

"I said *Jerrod* is the doctor on call."

She pawed at Sandy's arm, her eyes now wide

and her mind shocked into clarity." You can't let him in here. Please, Sandy, do something."

"But—"

Jerrod walked in. "Hello, I'm Doctor Carlson. I hear you're in lab—" His gaze froze on Hope's face. He glanced from her to Sandy and then back to Hope again. Confusion knitted his brows together.

"Hope…how? When? Who? He looked as though someone had ripped his heart out and handed it to him.

"Jerrod…" She gazed at him through a drugged haze. "Please save my baby. It's too soon."

He took hold of her hand. "Calm down. The medicine you've been given is supposed to relax you and stop the contractions. Appears it's working." He turned to the nurse. "May I have her chart, please?"

He glanced at Sandy. "I need you to step out while I examine Hope. I'll send someone to the waiting room to let you know when you can come back in."

Sandy nodded and left the room. Jerrod pulled a curtain around the cubicle and approached the bed. He leaned over Hope. "How far along are you?"

"S-seven months." Her voice quivered. At first she hadn't wanted this child, but now she wanted nothing more in her life - except maybe Jerrod, but it was too late for that. Unable to sit up, she grabbed his hand and yanked him closer. "Please, Jerrod, you have to save my daughter. She's all I have."

He stared into space, a blank look on his face, and then looked back at her. "We were together seven months ago." Tenseness ridged his jaw. "Is this my child?"

She started to answer, but pain stabbed at her stomach and overrode the medication. "Oh, help me." She pulled her knees up and curled into a ball, strained and straightened. "Something's wrong, Jerrod."

He tossed her chart aside, lifted the blanket and probed between her legs. He dropped the cover back into place, his expression strained. "Nurse, set up the delivery room, stat. We have a baby coming now!"

"No!" Hope screamed at the top of her lungs. "It's too soon."

Jerrod brushed the damp hair back from her forehead and soothed her brow. "Shhh, don't worry. Lot's of babies come early. Everything will be fine." He locked gazes with her. Hope, I have to know. Is this my child?"

His face blurred through tears. She nodded and then grabbed his sleeve. "I'm so sorry I didn't tell you, but...." She bit her lip as another wave of contractions washed over her.

"I'm anxious to hear your reason for keeping me in the dark, but I'll have to find out later. Right now, this little girl isn't going to wait."

"Can someone please let Sandy know?" Even in pain, Hope couldn't forget her best friend and her daughter's future Godmother.

****

Hope opened her eyes. Memories flooded back and she struggled to sit up, but large hands urged her back on her pillow. "Whoa now. Lay back and take it easy."

Her eyes widened on Jerrod. She touched her stomach. "My baby? Where's my baby?"

He sagged back in the bedside chair and ran a hand through his tousled hair. "*Our* daughter was born almost six hours ago. She's in the Neonatal Intensive Care Unit, and she's holding her own. You, on the other hand, lost quite a lot of blood in the process, and I've been worried about you.

"Have you been here the whole time?

He nodded. "There's nowhere else I'd rather be than by your side. I thought you knew that." He leaned forward and clasped her hand in his. "Why didn't you tell me about the baby, Hope?"

She turned her face to the wall. "I couldn't put you in that position."

"He rose, cupped her chin and forced her to look at him. "What position? Being a father? Raising a child with the woman I love? Why not?"

A lump formed in her throat. "You never told me you loved me until I broke things off. I was afraid you'd change your mind and think I got pregnant to trap you."

He released her hand, took a step back and stared at her, his eyes wide. "I wouldn't have thought that at all. I've always wanted to be a father."

"I had no idea." She knuckled a tear from her eye. "Can you forgive me?"

"It's not entirely your fault. I should have told you sooner how I felt about you. Is it too late for us? I really want to be part of my daughter's life...and her mother's, if she'll have me back." He brushed a kiss against her cheek.

"But, I've stolen so much time from you—from us."

He silenced her with two fingers to her lips. "Time starts now. Our daughter needs us both. Do you feel up to visiting her?"

"Oh, yes, I'd love that."

Jerrod scooped her into his arms and deposited her into the wheelchair parked in the corner. He tucked her gown around her legs, smiled, and spun her out into the hallway. "Do we know her name yet?"

Hope glanced over her shoulder. "I sort of like Danielle Ann." She turned her gaze forward and eyed the double doors they approached.

"Hmm, not bad."

She glanced back again. "After Dr. Daniel Smith. If he hadn't retired, I never would have met you. I think it's a perfect tribute."

"I like it." Jerrod paused and slapped a red button on the wall. The doors opened wide.

He wheeled her through, around a corner, and into a dimly lit room filled with incubators. Machines whirred and beeped, and somewhere across the way a baby cried—that sweet mewling sound only newborns make. Jerrod halted the chair in front of a shielded bassinet bearing the tag, "Baby Harrison."

With Jerrod supporting her elbow, Hope stood on weak legs and peered through the hood at her daughter—so small and fragile. "How much did she weigh?"

"Almost four pounds."

"She's so tiny." Hope's heart filled with a love she'd never before experienced. "I want to hold her."

"Okay, but first we need to settle something?"

"What?" She turned her face to him.

"I'll agree to Danielle as her first name, but you have to let me pick her last one."

Tears stung the back of Hope's eyes. "You mean—"

"Yes, I want to marry her mother. When we take our daughter home, she's going to have two parents committed to her…and to one another. Deal?"

Hope hooked her arm through Jerrod's and pulled him closer to the incubator. She bent over and peered at the precious baby inside. "Ms. Danielle

Carlson, I'd like you to meet your daddy. You're gonna love him because I know for sure, I do."

Really, The End

ALSO BY GINGER SIMPSON
FROM BOOKS WE LOVE

Destiny's Bride
Ellie's Legacy
Betrayed
First Degree Innocence
Special Edition
Sarah's Passion
Sarah's Heart
Time Invested
Time Tantrums
Culture Shock
A Novel Murder
Hattie's Heroes

NOTE FROM THE PUBLISHER

Thank you for purchasing and reading this Books We Love Book. We hope you have enjoyed your reading experience. Books We Love and the author would very much appreciate you returning to the online retailer where you purchased this book and leaving a review for the author.

Best Regards and Happy Reading,
Jamie and Jude

BOOKS WE LOVE AND
BOOKS WE LOVE SPICE
http://bookswelove.net

Top quality books loved by readers,
Romance, Mystery, Fantasy, Suspense
Vampires, Werewolves, Cops, Lovers.
Young Adult, Historical, Paranormal

For a spicier read visit
http://spicewelove.com